# What reviewers
# Dawson's previous novels:

"Last Rights is simply a gem..."

*—Vancouver Sun*

"Dawson has an innate flair for rhythm and characterization...."

*—The Hamilton Spectator*

"...a medical mindblower."

*—Publishers Weekly*

"...earn him respect as the author of both a superb mystery and a compelling novel."

*—Publishers Weekly*

"...a few wonderful and fully formed characters..."

*—The Boston Globe*

"David Laing Dawson's fans, including many who have read his medical thrillers in Dutch, German, French, Norwegian, Danish and Icelandic, will look forward to the next riveting adventure..."

*—The Ottawa Citizen*

"...beautifully paced, funny, and tense piece of crime writing."

"...most engaging new hero I've met in a long time."

"Dawson delivers a fast-paced and totally convincing story."

# I Swear to God

DAVID LAING DAWSON

One Printers Way
Altona, MB R0G 0B0
Canada

www.friesenpress.com


First Edition — 2024



ISBN
978-1-03-831935-7 (Hardcover)
978-1-03-831934-0 (Paperback)
978-1-03-831936-4 (eBook)

*1. FICTION, MYSTERY & DETECTIVE, WOMEN SLEUTHS*

Distributed to the trade by The Ingram Book Company

For Annaleigh

# Published Works

**Novels**

Last Rights
Double Blind
Essondale
The Intern
Slide in all Direction
Don't Look Down

**Non-fiction Books**

Schizophrenia in Focus
Relationship Management of the Borderline Patient
Two years of Trump on the Psychiatrist's Couch
The Adolescent Owner's Manual

**Plays**

Who Cares
The Waiting Room
Modern Times, Almost a Musical
The Decision
Assisted Living
MacBush, The Musical
Here Not There
If There is a River
Walter
I'm Here
Socks (short skit)

**Short Story Collection**

The Butterscotch Palace

**Film & Video**

My Name is Walter James Cross

Who Cares

Manic

Cutting For Stone

Schizophrenia in Focus

Painting with Tom, David, and Emily

The Brush, The Pen, and Recovery

Dead Anyway (co-writer)

**Poetry Collections**

Painting is Silent Poetry

A Feathered Symmetry

Love in the Time of COVID

Painting and Poetry

# One

"Any allergies?"

"Not that I'm aware of. 'Cept maybe to warm beer and cold women." Lying on the gurney, he looked over at her, smiled a little, then looked away and groaned.

"What about to medication, antibiotics, Demerol?" Sharon wrapped the cuff around his upper arm, covering the barbwire tattoo, and pushed the button to inflate, sat on the stool to wait for it.

He said, "I can take 'em all, no problem." And again grimaced and let out a howl of pain.

She was thinking about the tattoo. The one on his arm and the snake curling up the side of his neck from beneath the collar of his shirt. The man was tall, thin through his body, but wide shoulders, maybe thirty-five. She'd been telling her own kids these tats might look cool when you're playing high school volleyball, but not so hot you're talking with someone in human resources at IBM. On the other hand, even some of the young docs had tattoos these days. Shouldn't make a quick judgment about it. The LCD read 150 over 90 with a pulse of 86. She entered these in his newly created chart. He had short black hair, gelled up the sides to a spiky brush cut. The kind looked fine on Justin Timberlake, but not so good on a forty-year-old trying to stay young. No track marks in the crook of the one elbow she could see.

He said, "I'm dying here. When do I get to see the doc?"

"You're a long way from dying, Mr. Waverly."

"Well, excuse me for overstating the case. But there are some say kidney stones are the worst possible pain." He grimaced and groaned, pulled his knees up and turned his head away to make his point.

She said, taking her time, "Any blood in the urine?"

"Yes." He told her. "Yes. Bright red. Owwwww. Must be in my wha'd'yacallit."

"Your ureter."

"Right. Feels like glass in there. Shards of glass."

She was thinking, *Shards? Where would he get that word?*

She stood up, put the cuff away, "I'll get the doctor for you. You might want to strip to your jockeys and see if you can pass a little urine in this cup." She handed him a covered plastic container from the tray and pulled back the sliding glass door to let herself out. She turned halfway and said, with a little shrug, "But let me tell you, labour is worse. Especially the last part."

He watched her through the glass, walking toward the nursing station. He was thinking, *Shit personality but a nice ass on her.*

It was a quiet night so far, with the exception of this guy she just triaged, some leftovers from day and evening shift, waiting for beds or trips back to nursing homes, and the other man the intern was seeing.

Sharon wasn't sure if thinking that particular thought, "It's a quiet night," would do it, or if you had to say it out loud to bring down the wrath of God in a deluge of burst appendices, head-on car accidents, severed arms, heart attacks and strokes. She reached out to touch wood, stopped herself, looked at the clock on the wall. Three-thirty. Three and a half hours to go on the night shift.

She found Dr. Zabodny in the small alcove with the coffee urn, the one filled once a day with that terrible syrup the hospital cafeteria bought in large cans from a wholesaler of generally inedible products. The one urn lasted a full day as each shift brought in their own Timmy's, avoiding the hospital supply until late shift desperation. But Zabodny was drinking it. He had completed a rotation in emergency in July, she remembered. Scared shitless but covering it with that particular air of world-weariness the young docs assumed, adjusting their stethoscopes to hang just so around their shoulders, not yet aware the most important consideration would be a comfortable pair of shoes that wouldn't smell after eighteen hours walking the unforgiving floors of the hospital. That, and listening carefully to the experienced nurses. He was more relaxed now, in April, nine months of interning under his belt. He no longer had that look of a deer caught in the headlights.

He glanced up, said, "I can see you're in no hurry, so I can tell you what I just went through."

She put a mug under the urn, half filled it, added three sweeteners, and five of those annoying thimbles of two percent, sniffing one of them first.

He watched her do this, said, "You wouldn't believe it, the guy I just saw. He's coming home from the evening shift at Dofasco. Figures it's time to get his ears cleaned. Seems he has unusual amounts of wax buildup. Tells me it's hereditary. Also, he's on permanent afternoons, nights, so he sleeps all day, and can't get to appointments when the sun is up. Figures the emergency ward is a twenty-four-hour service, so drops in. Says if he saw a lot of ambulances coming in, he'd have passed. So that's it. He comes to the emergency of the General Hospital, the trauma centre, would you believe it, for wax build up. He wants his ears cleaned. Did I forget to say 'fucking'? He wants his fucking ears cleaned."

Sharon remembered he'd had a slight Slavic accent back in July. Almost undetectable now. Thought, *Maybe it goes away he's relaxed.* Sitting down, grimacing over the coffee, leaving the new chart on her lap, she said, "So what'd you do?"

"I syringed his ears."

"Get a lot of wax?"

"Yeah."

"Use ice-cold water?"

He said, "That would have been sweet."

"It's not Dofasco anymore."

"I know. But Ancelor-Mittal just doesn't have the same ring to it." He reached for the chart, and she gave it to him as he said, "What's the story on the guy you got in eleven?"

"Renal colic. Stones."

"And you're not in a hurry?"

"I don't buy it."

"Why? Is he a regular?"

She noticed he was showing a little experience. Not getting huffy like some, especially the new female interns, saying something like, "Isn't that for me to decide?"

She said, "No. I haven't seen him before. Says one of his friends dropped him off. He was at a house party and collapsed in pain."

"And?"

"BP, pulse slightly elevated. Says there's blood in his urine."

"So what makes you think he's not kosher?"

"I guess it's his eyes."

"His eyes?"

"Uh huh."

"What about his eyes?"

"He's in as much pain as he says he wouldn't be looking me over so...carefully."

Zabodny smiled, said, "You mean undressing you with his eyes?"

She handed him the chart. "You better take a look at him. See if he pricked his finger to get some blood in his urine."

Taking the chart in hand and leaving, he said, "Where's the love and compassion?"

She saw the waiting room was filling up when she came back from another triage, this time a head injury she had quickly handed to the surgical staff, the chief resident on call. IV in place, catheterized, portable oxygen, she was on her way for an MRI. Just a kid, sixteen, a passenger in the car of an eighteen-year-old drunk who got away with a broken wrist. Zabodny was writing in the chart she had given him earlier.

He looked up, said, "There was blood in his urine, and he says he's in a lot of pain. Very tender in the right kidney area. I'll have to give him some pethidine while we're waiting on the MRI. Think you can get an IV started?"

She could let this run its course. She knew it wouldn't make much difference in the big scheme of things. But something about the sixteen-year-old she just saw, the victim, she was sure, of some goddamn boy high on God knows what driving Daddy's car. A girl who could be her own daughter in a few years. She said, "Let me take him some pills. Just give me a minute. If I'm wrong, I'm wrong."

He said, "If you're wrong, what do I get?"

He was flirting with her, almost young enough to be her son, if she had given birth at fifteen, say. She said, "Next shift, I'll bring you a Tim Horton's and you won't have to drink that shit."

"I don't mind it. Something like my oma used to make. You couldn't use the good spoons in it 'cause the silver would melt off. But if you've got this guy nailed, what would you want from me?" There he was, flirting again.

"Eternal gratitude, Dr. Zee. Eternal gratitude."

He said, "I'm always grateful you don't let me make a fool of myself."

She took Advil from her own purse, paused a moment, then put it on a small tray with a glass of orange juice from the refrigerator, and carried these down the hall to room eleven. She could see the waiting room was filling up, a small lineup at the reception, could hear an ambulance coming this way, down Barton. The three nurses were busy, the chief resident calling orders around a gurney being wheeled past. She decided all you had to do was think "It's a quiet night" to test fate.

As she pulled back the sliding door, she said, "How are you doing now, Mr. Waverly?"

He was sitting on the edge of the gurney in his jockey shorts and socks, shirt on but unbuttoned. He said, "Doc, order me something for the pain?"

She said, "Well, here's the thing, Mr. Waverly. See how busy it is out there?" She placed the small square tray beside the bed. "Seems we're totally out of pethedine and Demerol. New shipment won't be in until nine or later."

He said, "What about some oxy? A shot of morphine?"

"That too. Nothing. The cupboard's bare. I brought you some Advil should help."

"Advil?"

"Advil. Super strength."

"Advil."

"Advil. Take two with some of this juice." She shook two caplets out of the container.

He looked at her, said, "Jesus Christ. You're serious?"

"I'm serious. It's a real problem, these shortages, budget cuts."

"Lady, I'm dying here."

"I don't think so, Mr. Waverly."

He eased himself off the gurney with some agility, started pulling his pants on, then his shoes, muttering, "I don't believe this shit."

She noticed he was moving easily with no signs of pain, waited for him. He had his pants on now, shirt tucked in, shoes on but unlaced.

He looked at her, a step too close, looked into her eyes, said, "You're a cold cunt, you know that? A cold cunt."

She knew to just stand there, hold his eyes, not say anything, not move, not smile. For a split second, she wondered if she had gone too far. Maybe she should have let the thing run its course, given the man his fix. It was not as if this little intervention was going to make much of a dent in the rate of addiction to prescription narcotics.

His fist clenched, unclenched. But he grabbed his jacket, went out the sliding glass door and headed down the hall toward the waiting area, offering one last "Fuck" to the ceiling tiles.

She followed to watch him leave, keeping her distance. As he went through the waiting area, she heard him ask someone who looked like an industrial accident, in work clothes, left hand bound up in thick, bloody towelling, "Hey, buddy, which way to the Catholic hospital from here?"

He didn't wait for an answer, headed for the main entrance, saying loudly over his shoulder, "Where they just might give a shit."

She could see him through the glass doors, outside, now on his cell. She asked herself why she bothered. He'd get what he was looking for somewhere. She remembered what that twelve-year-old girl had told her when she'd asked, "How on earth does someone your age get hold of cocaine and OxyContin?"

The girl had said, "It's easy. You just go downtown, look for any scruffy guy standing around a corner, go up and ask if he's holding." Of course, you have to have money to buy, or something to sell. There had been a period in her own life when she found the pams taking over, lorazepam, oxazepam, diazepam, clonazepam, after Hamish left, when it took one to sleep, then two, then three, then another to calm the morning jitters. Until she got angry at her own dependence and weaned herself off.

She joined Zabodny, who was at the side of a gurney the paramedics had just brought in. An older woman was lying on the gurney. She was flat, pale, had sunken eyes. She was not responding to their words or their touch, not sweaty, dry skin, not in visible pain, shallow breathing but breathing with no obstruction, her pulse weak. Sharon took all this in as she searched for, found a vein, and started the IV.

He pulled the stethoscope from his ears, said to her, with a lot more self-assurance than he had had in July, she noticed, "Internal bleed. Probably stomach, GI."

She pulled the sheet back covering the woman's legs, saw some dark red leakage, a terrible mix of feces and blood, and simply said, "Looks that way."

He was taking blood from the other arm for crossmatch, squirting it into a tube, when he said, "And the guy in eleven? I saw him leaving us. Advil did the trick, huh?"

"Eternal gratitude, Dr. Zee. Eternal gratitude."

He said, "Maybe you'll get a medal from the premier, cutting down the wait time."

# Two

Jerome found his car where he'd left it, parked on a side street up from the hospital. He kicked the passenger door before getting in. He knew some of the losers who worked the emergency wards and urgent care centres to get a little product. Mostly, they were sick bastards, faking seizures but sometimes really had seizures, faking pain but really had bad livers, DTs, most of their brain cells gone except for the sneaky ones. And migraines. That worked for the women. Go in with migraine headaches, get a shot of Demerol or morphine. Migraines didn't work for guys nearly as well. Guy claims he's got a blinding headache, can't see, they figure he's a fake or a wuss. And there was no point over-acting, yelling and screaming; they'd just put you down with some Zydis dissolved in the mouth before you could spit it out, or a shot of Haldol in the ass. What the hell was he trying this for? He wasn't that desperate. What a waste of time. But that doc was gonna give him something before the bitch nurse got in the way.

Sitting in his car, figuring what to do next, he felt himself coming down; he could feel that foggy hollow in his chest, little electric shocks in his brain. By morning, the world would look like a toilet to puke in.

He didn't really have to ask directions to the Catholic hospital, St. Joseph's, but last time he looked, there was a sign just inside the door of their emergency department: "We do not renew narcotic prescriptions," cutting off the scam before it started, telling the emergency doc you left your pills on the bus, or your girlfriend swiped them, or your family doc retired, or you accidentally spilled them in the sink. Then there was this gizmo, same as you'd find at an old-time deli, a spool of tickets with numbers on each one. All busted up in some kind of emergency, you were expected to take a ticket and sit quietly until your number was called. "Thirty-seven." Also flashing across an LCD. Then, if you could walk, you'd have to go into this little room that had a nurse in there doing triage, taking down the information and deciding if anybody should hurry, or let you wait another six hours.

Why bother?

He was sitting in his Civic, passenger window with new glass in it, but stuck a couple of inches down, not sure what to do next, honestly a little ashamed he'd tried the kidney stone scam to get a single fix. He's not that big a loser. But damn, the doc was gonna fix him up till that bitch nurse got into it.

He started the piece of crap car. He hadn't really expected his Civic to be still drivable when he got out of jail, parked in his mother's front yard through two winters. Just sitting there, tires flat, battery dead. His mother had said, "Don't you drive before you've got a licence and insurance."

He'd told her, after he'd got it turning over. "Only to my probation appointments and NA. How else am I gonna get there?"

Pulling onto Sanford, he figured he might as well go home, try to ride it out. He had no money, nothing to sell. Or plan B, what he'd been avoiding. This jerk he met in the can had a setup on Upper Wentworth, selling to the teenagers. He'd said, "Christ, you can't trust teenagers. Rat you out for a soda pop." The guy had said, "No." Actually, what he'd said was, "*Al contrario*, the little buggers live by the code they pick up from gangster movies, don't talk to cops, never rat out a friend. They know they're not gonna do time anyway."

Jerome had said, "But they got no money."

The guy had said, "Are you kidding? Their mommas give them plenty, they pawn shit, and the ones don't have enough deal half of what they buy to the kids got money but are too chicken to get it directly. It's sweet."

He hadn't asked if it's so sweet how come he's in here doing six months, six months in the Barton Jail, the Hamilton Detention Centre. He didn't like the guy. Asshole had come right up to him and said, "So you shot your poppa. How come you only got two years less a day? I'm just asking 'cause I'm thinking of firing my lawyer's ass. And yours must be pretty good."

Short, greasy little bugger, says he come from El Salvador. Jerome asked why'd they put him in jail, why not deport his ass, and the guy tells him, "Torture, man. They send me back, they put me in a cell and pull out my fingernails. Maybe they make me disappear. Here, I do the time, out in three months. Your government don't like torture, man. Don't want the newspapers saying they sent a freedom fighter to have his cajónes electrocuted. You people's the most guilty in the world, man. Like this kid they got in Guantanamo, goes to Afghanistan to shoot Americans, and now the Americans're asking him questions without his momma holding his hand, and you watch the TeeVee he's got Canadians feeling so bad for him. Y'know, you bump into a civilian in the street, he says sorry, like he's apologizing for breathing. That's guilt. What we call *sentido de culpa*. And you can wonder where it came from, or you can take advantage of it. One or the other."

Jerome is trying to think of his real name, everybody calling him Sal. He decides, "What the hell?" He can hear his mother's voice saying, "Beggars can't be choosers," as he turns the Civic up Wentworth, figures he'll look the guy up, see what he has. A partner can speak Spanish wouldn't be so bad, deal with the Colombians directly. Nothing's for keeps. Then he realizes, shit, it's four in the morning, decides to find an all-night Tim Horton's, get some sugar and sleep in the car till the sun comes up.

# Three

She gave report at seven, talking through it as quickly as possible. Didn't bother telling them the story of the addict who left so rudely. Only the ones still pending, holding, waiting for beds or blood results, needed watching. The day shift understood she had a couple of teenagers at home, and she needed to get there in time to send them off to school. Be a good parent and not feel that bad about being unavailable for ten hours at a time. Permanent nights seemed to work best for everybody; she could get her children home in the evening, pull them off TikTok and Instagram, confiscate cell phones, tuck them in, be back in time to haul them out of bed in the morning. Until recently at least, Christian taking to wandering in at all hours, saying he was over at Jaimie's playing video games and lost track of time, Sharon knowing it was a lie, Jaimie's mother not knowing where either of them was.

She checked her cell for messages before getting in her silver Jetta in the parking garage, the sun just coming up over the lakeside industry. There was a beauty to it, she had to admit. Getting off shift in the early morning, sun coming up over the lake, refracting red and yellow in the pollution coming from the steel mills.

She could make it home by seven forty-five, eight. In theory, they'd both be up and showered and she could have a coffee with them while they ate breakfast, Christian wolfing down anything and half a quart of milk, Alicia insisting on fruit and low-fat yogourt. And before taking herself to bed, she would be treated to their playful banter, such as it is: "You like suck, you know that, Dickweed." And, "Mom, will you please stop your son from being so gross? Like, can you hear him eat? It's disgusting." Didn't she just read a review of a book on the joys of being childless?

The other thing on her mind as she drove up the Jolly Cut against the traffic was her flirting with Zabodny and that other good-looking intern on the surgical rotation, both younger than herself by a good ten years. Not that she wanted to do it, or planned it in any way, just that she noticed it was happening. A few years ago, she would have thought it stupid, unseemly. But now they were all doing it, or so the tabloids said. These forty-year-old cougars with boy toys. Still, it was probably stupid. Did she really want an anxiety-ridden, overly serious young doctor in her bed? She smiled to herself, didn't answer her own question, decided to just .... And then she imagined Hamish coming to drop off the kids and finding her in bed with someone half his age. Her smile broadened as she pulled into the driveway.

She was picturing it as she unlocked the front door. Hamish would have a key, bring the kids back early, let himself in while they fetched their bags from the trunk of the car. He'd walk in the bedroom, see this young Adonis in bed with his ex-wife, say, "Excuse me, who the hell is that?" And she would say, "Hamish, I'd like you to meet"—what was his first name?—"George. I'd like you to meet George." Or maybe she should pronounce it *Sheorgi.*

Make it sound more exotic. And Sheorgi Zabodny would say, "What the hell kind of name is Hamish?" And she'd tell him how his parents wanted a boy who'd fit into Upper Canada College. But that would probably be lost on Zabodny.

In the house, nobody was stirring. She took off her raincoat, put her purse on the kitchen table, and climbed the half stairs of the split-level to the bedroom area. Christian's bedroom door still had the "Do Not Enter" sign he'd glued to it three years ago. She knocked loudly first and then opened the door. She did her best to ignore the pile of clothes on the carpet, the open closet door, clothing spilling on the floor, empty pizza box, pop can, large running shoes piled in the corner, death metal poster. She focused on the bed and decided, yes, it hadn't been slept in. He'd been out all night doing God knows what.

With Christian being seventeen, she had, she knew, little leverage. The tough love books would tell her to set the rules, demand compliance or else. The "else" being kicked out. Put out on the street where he'd be sure to avoid school and seek the company of other teens in similar predicaments. And Hamish would have a lot to say about it, short of taking the kid in himself. So, what choice did she really have? Except to make sure he had a bed to sleep in, a refrigerator to eat from, his mother's admonitions ringing in his ears every time he sucked on a bong or whatever the hell else they were doing. And controlling the money. Controlling the money, she reminded herself. She'd have to count her CDs again, check her jewellery, see if anything was missing.

She knocked on Alicia's door and listened to the muffled, "What? What? Do you have to be so loud?" and then, "Oh my God. Oh my God. Do you see what time it is?"

Sharon said, "Get your buns in the bathroom, my sweet. I'll have breakfast ready."

She liked her kitchen. Big enough for a breakfast table, the coffee maker, refrigerator handy, back door opening onto a small garden, lots of light. One smart thing she did was buy a house for herself and the kids right after they separated, close to the school they'd be going to, in a neighbourhood with rising real estate value. Hamish had wanted her to stay in the matrimonial (she had come to hate that word) home, leave it in joint ownership, not disrupt the children's lives. That was his rationale. Said in that tone of voice, the presentation of superior logic: "We should try to disrupt the children's lives as little as possible." She suspected he had a fantasy of having the wife and kids, all very domestic, big pot of stew on the stove, ironing board loaded with clean clothes, old sheep dog lying under the table, in a big ramshackle farmhouse on 10 acres in the country. He could come and go as he pleased while enjoying a separate life in the city with his cronies and his paramour. Telling tall tales to his mates in the gentlemen's club, sipping on a glass of claret. His name was Victorian, so why not his fantasies?

It was 8:30 by the time Alicia emerged from the bathroom, eye shadow applied, hair straightened. She had been examining herself in the mirror, said, "I think I need one more ring in my left ear."

Sharon ignored this. She had cut up some strawberries for both of them, mixed with Yoplait. Precisely a half glass of orange juice for Alicia, which would be precisely all she would drink, and had placed beside the glass, a vitamin D tablet and an omega-3 capsule. She said, "Your brother didn't come home last night?"

"Must you refer to him that way? I prefer to think of him as a refugee we had to take in from Kazakhstan."

She said, "I see you're wearing black, again." She didn't want to push the issue. At least her daughter's midriff was covered, no thighs or décolletage in sight.

Daintily nibbling on the strawberries and yogourt, as if eating too quickly would cause her to balloon, she said, in response, Sharon supposed, to her observation, "There's a girl at my school. She says she and her mother are both Wiccans."

"How nice for them."

"My point being, Mother..." But she seemed to have lost her point. Drinking down the orange juice, she said, "I'll be late unless you drive me."

Sharon could hear herself saying, "And whose fault is that?" but suppressed this. "Did he call, leave a message, anything?"

She said, "Nada. You expect too much from men, Mother. If you would lower your expectations, you wouldn't be so disappointed."

Sharon remembered this age, so righteous, moral, superior. So certain of everything and so uncertain at the same time. Charming and clever, too. She said, "I'm worried about him."

Alicia looked up for a second, revealing a smidgen of sisterly concern, then she said, "Well, if anything serious had happened to him, you'd already know, right?"

"That's true." She got up from the table, thinking about the sixteen-year-old with head injury brought to the trauma centre last night. She said, "C'mon, grab your books. I'll drive you."

As she was getting in the car, Alicia on the other side waiting for the door to unlock, Sharon said, "You know, last night in emergency, a man called me a cold cunt. Would you believe it?"

Alicia looked over the roof of the car, said, "Mother, please don't use the c-word." When she was settled in the passenger seat, Sharon turning the ignition, Alicia added, "Is he still alive?"

She had dropped her daughter off and watched for a minute as her little girl hurried up the main walkway to the school's front entrance. She had said, unnecessarily, as she pulled up, "You're late." Alicia had reassured her she had a spare first class. "Don't sweat it," she'd said as she stepped out of the car, grabbing her pack from the back seat.

On the way home, Sharon considered picking up a Starbucks, decided it would keep her awake, and then she was caught in traffic, the last-minute rush. She thought, *Maybe he'll be there by the time I get home, behaving like there's nothing unusual about pulling in at nine in the morning after an all-nighter.* And then be indignant as she tries to talk with him, saying he's got to get some sleep, have a heart. If she reams him out, she won't be able to sleep herself. She decided to ignore the situation until she'd had at least seven hours.

It was 9:30 before she got back home. There were no signs of dropped bags or clothing between the front door and the kitchen, nothing disturbed. She looked in his room and found it exactly as before. That was when the phone rang. Expecting it to be Christian with a lame excuse—hoping it would be Christian, actually—she was surprised by a woman's voice, calling her "Mrs. Gibson." The voice went on to say she was Ms. Darnell, vice principal of Lester B. Pearson, and she was calling to see if Mrs. Gibson knew how many classes her son Christian had missed this term. Sharon said, "I don't know exactly, but I'm sure it's quite a few."

Ms. Darnell said, "He's perilously close to suspension, Mrs. Gibson."

Sharon felt a surge of anger, her first thought being, *Good idea. Kid doesn't want to go to school, you punish him by suspending him.* But she held her tongue, said, "I'm doing my best to get him there."

Ms. Darnell said, "I'd like to meet with you, see what we can do. And his father, of course."

Sharon didn't say anything at first, not knowing how to respond, what to tell her.

Ms. Darnell then added, "There may be other problems as well."

A weariness settled in as Sharon said, simply, "Okay. What time would work for you? I've been on the night shift. I need to get a little sleep first."

They agreed on 5:00 p.m., her office, not far from the main entrance, just past the general office.

Sharon sat for a minute after hanging up. Then she went to her bedroom, made sure the blinds and curtains blocked out most of the sunlight, turned on a fan to drown out street noises, crawled into bed. Finding herself wide awake, she decided she'd have to resort to Imovane. She shook out a small oval pill from the bottle beside her bed, broke it in half, put one half back in the vial and swallowed the other as quickly as possible. It still left a bitter taste in her mouth.

# Four

"You di'n' tell me why you killed your poppa."

Jerome said, "It's hard to explain."

"It's okay, brother. My own poppa, he needed shooting, but I was too young to do it the time I left."

It was embarrassing, Jerome was thinking, not being able to remember the guy's last name, thinking of him as Sal Mineo, old-time greaser actor came to a sad end, the guy being friendly enough. They were sitting in the main room of his apartment, Jerome pulling on a joint the guy had offered, letting his nerves settle. He was thinking the dump must have come furnished, or the guy had a truckload from the Sally Ann delivered, it was that bad. It had taken him all morning to find the place, a low rise on Upper Wentworth, and then he'd had to try a few buttons, first initial S. Finally got the guy who answered suspiciously, "Yes?"

Salvatore Minero, that was his name. Jerome had said, "Yeah, it's Jerome. We met maybe three months ago." Telling him the time frame they were in the joint together.

The voice on the intercom had said, simply, "Yes."

Jerome said, "Just in the neighbourhood, man, dropping by, you know."

"I don' know," said the voice, but he buzzed Jerome in.

Now Sal noticed Jerome looking the place over. He said, "I make the place pretty and my PO drops by, she wonder how I pay for it. This way, no problem." He had given Jerome a beer, a Corona, found a couple of joints in a sugar jar, beckoned him to sit on the overstuffed couch with the frayed armrests.

He said, "You found me how?"

Jerome explained he remembered Sal telling him he knew he'd get six months, out in three, had paid for his apartment on Upper Wentworth in advance. There weren't that many of them.

Sal said, "And you look me up because?" Watching him, curious, the guy tall, a little muscle on him now, a tough guy tat up his neck, slim hips, sucking on the joint like he had a pain needed fixing.

Jerome said, "I see you're on your own. Could use a partner, maybe."

That's when Sal said, "You di'n' tell me why you killed your poppa."

Jerome was itching to tell him about the other thing they never got him for, shooting the Black dude, but decided maybe he'd use that later if he ever had to impress the guy. He said, "My old man needed shooting a long time ago, just out himself for manslaughter, and I catch him beating up the old lady."

Sal said, "Ah, tha's why you get two years less a day. They don't like that here, a man hits his wife."

Jerome said, "Yeah, and my lawyer made sure lots of women on the jury. Let them know what a bad man he was, my poppa. They near to giving me a medal the way my lawyer tells it. And they might have let me off I'd of hit him with a frying pan 'stead of fetching a piece and putting a bullet in his ass."

Sal said, "What's your momma think about it, you shooting her old man?"

"That's a puzzlement," said Jerome. "He's beat the crap out of her, did it many times before, now he's gone, she's crying and weeping, telling me I'll go straight to hell for what I did. That was at first. Then she come around. Took a couple of months in the OH to get her through it."

"The OH?" says Sal.

"I believe you people call it the *Casa des Locos*," said Jerome, showing off. Seeing Sal's big smile, he added, "You got any blow to go with this?" He had sucked the joint to a small roach, still trying to get something from it.

Sal looked at him, said, "I don't keep no product here. That would be stupid. Maybe a gram of weed. My PO doesn't care, and I don't give the cops a cause to search. And I don't give it away, either. You think you can earn it?"

Jerome said, "Could be. But what I see here is a poor man got nothing to offer." He was aware the cannabis was making him a little reckless, but what the hell, see what the greaser does with it.

Sal was looking him over. This was clearly not a smart one, but maybe what he needed. Alone he was vulnerable, had to keep a low profile, deal with fucking teenagers. He tries to expand his territory. The bikers come visiting, or the Jamaicans. When he moved to Hamilton, he was told it would be a Guinea at the door, a no-neck talking like he grew up in New York, telling him he had a message from Johnny Pops, or one of the Musitanos, but they'd fucked each other over, lost control, and now it would be some guy on a Harley he tries to deal on Upper James, or a slow talking Rastafarian he tries Lower James, the territories shifting a little each month, but keeping the peace so far. He said, "Don' get fool by appearances. Like you, man. Who believe you a killer? Huh?"

Jerome was holding in a last deep drag. Letting it out, all he could say was, "That's fucking A."

Sal said, "I have business to attend to today. You come back tomorrow, we talk some more. Maybe you can help me, maybe not."

"I got ideas," says Jerome. He was thinking, *Maybe the guy's got nothing going, or maybe something.* They could dance a little longer.

"I'm sure you have," said Sal, getting to his feet, walking to the door, rolling his shoulders a little.

Jerome wanted to look around, see if it was true the guy kept no product here. And if not here, where? But he could bide his time, see how it played out. Or follow him, see where he had his stash. He said, "Yeah. Lots of 'em. But I better go check on my momma, see she's feeding herself."

Sal said, "It's a responsibility, your momma." And ushered him out. It was a nondescript corridor, every door looking the same in this four-storey brick. He was thinking of just sitting in his Civic and watching the front entrance, see where Sal was going, if he was going anywhere.

As he left the building, a teenager with a ball cap covering shifty eyes squeezed past him going in, another standing outside trying to look like he owned the street. Jerome suddenly felt very hungry, only beer in his stomach so far today. He changed his mind about sitting and watching; he knew he'd never have the patience for it, get distracted by the first half-decent-looking chick walks by. It was clouding over, maybe going to rain. He drove down the mountain and out to the east end. He'd see what was in his momma's refrigerator.

# Five

Pulling out of the driveway, she did the math in her head: asleep by maybe ten, up at four, which meant six hours tops, still groggy with the bitter taste of the sleeping pill lingering. And Christian had not come home at all. No phone calls either. She tried his cell phone and was put through to voice mail. When Alicia came in the kitchen door just after four, she had suggested checking his Facebook page, see if he had left a clue. But Sharon had explained she had to go to a meeting with his teachers first. Maybe they could check the internet later. She had said she should be back by 6:30 at the latest. And then, in one of those rare moments of adolescent empathy, Alicia had noticed her mother's weariness, and had said, "I'll make supper for us. I'll have it ready by the time you get back."

Which might mean, of course, Sharon knew, that Alicia had plans for the evening and didn't want her mother's appointment to make her late. Her own parents, what would they do if their son, her brother, didn't come home, with no Facebook, cell phones? Wait forty-eight, seventy-two hours and call the cops? Maybe. But, more likely, her father would announce that the kid would drag his sorry ass home eventually, when his money runs out. Then, go on to point out he worked the oil rigs at that age, and his father left home at sixteen, and his grandfather was squatting in a trench at Vimy the same age. Time the kid grew up. She knew the first story was true, her father working a man's job by the time he was seventeen, but her great-grandfather must have been a few years past that when he sat in a trench at Vimy Ridge. So what was different now?

At the first red light, Sharon took her cell phone from her purse and dialled with her right thumb while holding the steering wheel with her left hand, trying to watch both the phone and the light. The light changed just as she finished and pushed speaker. Hamish would be at the office, she was sure, and after 4:30, with any luck, she wouldn't have to go through his secretary.

He picked up, had read the call display, said, "Sharon?"

"It's me. I thought you might want to know I'm on my way to see the VP of the school about your son skipping classes."

"Are you on a cell?"

"Yes. What's that got to do with it?"

"And driving?"

"Did you hear anything I said?"

"You shouldn't be driving and talking. It's illegal now, didn't you notice?"

"He didn't come home last night either."

"He didn't call, tell you where he is?"

"No. And this is the third time. Shit."

"What?"

"Okay. I'm at a stop sign. I said this is not the first time."

There was silence for a moment. Then, "I'll talk to him on the weekend."

"I think it needs more than a talk."

"Well, what do you want me to do?"

"I was thinking more like scare some sense into him. He doesn't listen to me."

"He's seventeen."

"I know he's seventeen. I have to go. I'll be late."

"I'll talk to him this weekend."

"If we find him alive."

"What?"

"Never mind. Gotta go." She closed the cell and drove across the intersection. She was aware of her ambivalence. She needed help with Christian, but she didn't want to sound helpless. She didn't need Hamish trying to calm her, reassure her. And she wasn't sure if she was frightened for Christian or wanted to wring his skinny neck. At least she hadn't had to ask the secretary for permission to speak with her ex-husband.

Getting into the car, Sharon had been aware of unseasonably humid air and dark clouds rolling in from the west. And now thunder grumbled in the distance and rain suddenly splashed on her windshield as she pulled into the visitors parking on the west side of Pearson Secondary. *It's too early in the season for this*, she was thinking, *but then, all bets are off with global warming*. She fished amid debris in the back seat on the off chance she'd left an umbrella there. Nothing. The rain came harder, then eased. Holding a folded newspaper over her head, she hurried from the parking lot to the main walkway.

It was an imposing building, almost a city block wide, three stories in yellow brick, high windows, some gothic flourishes to the decorative cornices, a large main entrance up a flight of cement steps. Just inside the double doors, she dumped the wet newspaper in a blue box, then shed her coat to shake off the surface water. The lighting was poor, with little coming from outside. She looked at the information panel directly ahead, and at the banners announcing homecoming, and to the right of this a glass display wall of trophies.

To both her left and right, wide corridors and terrazzo floors led past lockers and doors to classrooms until they came to stairs going down to side doors and up to the second floor. Nothing stirred to her right, but in the distance on her left, silhouetted by light from the side door, a figure appeared briefly and then disappeared down the flight of stairs to the door. She could see no details, but the boy's legs, his movements...like his father's...the same shape and rhythm. She knew she could have imagined this. She realized while driving to the school she had been watching for Christian on each street corner she passed.

She put the thought out of her mind and walked toward what appeared to be the main office, with a list of offices within on a board to the left of the double glass door. The list included Vice Principal P. Darnell. She didn't know Ms. Darnell's first name, wondered if it was some old-fashioned Prudence or Philomena. She found the outer office deserted, the secretaries gone, their desks behind the counter tidied up. To her right would be the principal's office. To her left, logically, the vice principal's.

The door with an opaque etched glass upper panel was slightly ajar. She knocked on it. No response. She stepped back to check the number on the lower panel. She shrugged, pushed the door open, walked in.

To her right was a wooden desk, behind this a window looking out on schoolyard and playing fields. And beside the desk, sprawled on the floor, strangely curled, was a woman. Sharon blinked. She looked out at the playing field, noticed the rain had let up and some kids were trying to get a softball game going. She took a step forward, wondering if the woman had just now fallen, or fainted. Her ER mind ran through a quick differential: heart attack, stroke, head injury, seizure, low blood sugar...and then she saw the blood. Her shoes were in it, a puddle spreading out from under the woman toward the centre of the room. She stepped backward, walked backwards out of the room. She found herself looking at the number on the door once again, incongruously assuring herself she was in the right room. Then she spun around and clutched the countertop. She gagged, took a deep breath. She dropped her wet coat and purse on the counter and went back in the room. She was an emergency nurse, after all; the woman might be alive.

Trying to avoid the pool of blood, aware this was too late, and realizing she may have spoken to this woman only eight hours earlier, she bent down to feel for a carotid pulse. But Sharon had seen death before and knew this to be it. She pulled herself up, walked back to the main office, pushed through the partial swing door into the secretaries' area, found a phone, and dialled 911. Once she had told the operator her name and what she was reporting, she slumped back in a chair, bowed her head, and tried to think of this as an unrelated occurrence, an accident, a medical misfortune. But she was aware the blood had not come from the woman's mouth, nose, or bowels, the usual sources for a hemorrhage related to illness. She seemed to have bled from her chest or abdomen.

"Alicia, I'm sorry. You'll have to make your own supper tonight...I don't know. No. Nothing to do with Chris." She glanced up from the phone on the secretary's desk to the detective watching her.

He had been listening to her phone call, not intently, but listening for sure. They had taped off the scene, waiting for the MO, the uniform cops just securing everything before the detectives arrived. This one had introduced himself as Detective Nash and had started writing down her statement when she insisted on calling her fourteen-year-old daughter, who was home alone.

She listened to Alicia, thought how fleeting that moment of empathy had been, and said into the phone, "No. You may not go out tonight. You just sit there and wait for me. And if Chris shows up, tell him to just sit down and wait as well...I know. Do it anyway. I'll get home as soon as I can."

Detective Nash had stayed a few discrete feet away. Now, he sat on the edge of the desk and reopened his small pad. She wondered why they took notes in those tiny little books, big masculine printing trying to fit verbatim comments on a few lines. He was saying, "So, you had an appointment with Ms. Darnell at 5:00 p.m., and you were a few minutes late. No one was in the outer office. You walked in and found her just the way she is now."

"I'm afraid I stepped in the blood. And I, well actually, I backed out, caught my breath and then went back in and checked her pulse."

"Checked her pulse?"

"I'm a nurse. I felt for a carotid pulse."

"And that's why you're relatively calm about all this?"

"Pardon me?"

"Don't take it the wrong way. I'm just saying you're fairly

composed because you're a nurse."

She wasn't sure if that had been a statement or a question. She said, "An emergency nurse at the General."

"Ahhh."

It was usually the uniform cops who brought people in, waited for them if they were going from hospital to jail or court. The ER nurses and police had a sort of front-line bond, the cops very protective. She remembered being pulled over for speeding once, the cop waving her on after discovering she was an ER nurse, his explanation being, "I don't wanna arrive in your ER one day with a bullet wound and have you thinking, 'That's the bastard gave me a speeding ticket.'" Like it was inevitable, often on his mind.

Nash was scribbling something. Then he looked up from his notepad and asked, "And the appointment was about?"

"My son. Christian. He's been skipping classes lately. Like all of them these days." She hesitated, heard herself defending him.

"Was he supposed to be at the appointment, too?"

"No. Just me. As far as I know."

"You asked for the appointment, or Ms. Darnell?"

"She called this morning. Told me about Chris skipping classes. Asked for a meeting."

Nash said, "I'm impressed. I didn't think they cared anymore. My own kid, you know how I found out he was playing hooky? Vice was looking at some surveillance tape from that video place downtown. They call me over, 'Harry, take a look at this. You see any major felons?' And there he was. Two in the afternoon and my kid is a mile from school playing *Grand Theft Auto*."

She didn't say anything. Thought about his first name being Harry.

Nash said, "So the meeting was just you alone?"

Sharon said, "As far as I know."

"And where might he be now? Your kid, I mean."

She had answered him. And she hadn't lied. But she was aware of some motherly instinct kicking in, circling the wagons. She had said, "He should be at home. And I should be there too."

Nash had let it go. He'd said, "It's gonna be a zoo around here. Tonight, tomorrow. You might want to slip out before the reporters and television get here."

She had thanked him and left by a side door, ignoring the arrival of a van brimming with antennae and satellite dishes. It was still light. The clouds had cleared, the rain stopped. In any other circumstances, it would have been a beautiful spring evening.

Driving home, her mind kept drifting to an image of the boy at the end of the corridor, in silhouette, the stride, his shape, edges of the silhouette distorted by the light from the side door, dropping from view as he loped down the stairs. *It could have been anyone,* she told herself, *and totally unrelated. What were there? Twelve hundred kids attending that school? Six hundred boys? It couldn't be possible. They all wear the same thing. Ball cap, baggy pants, sneakers.* She found herself breathing shallowly, gasping for air. She was grateful for a red light and a chance to calm herself.

# Six

The security guard had been on the third floor, doing his rounds, checking each classroom for stragglers, locking up. He hadn't heard a thing unusual, he said, until the sirens. A few kids were still in the gym with a teacher, nobody on the main floor. Three possible exits: out the main entrance, or the two side doors at each end of the corridor. These had been locked for coming in, but the crash bars allowed egress. Nash had been explaining this to Dobrowski after he arrived, apologizing he'd been picking his own kid up from St. Thomas More, his ex's day to get the kid, but she'd phoned saying she was tied up. They were on the front steps, looking around, a uniformed cop barring entrance to the school, a TV crew setting up camera and microphone, ready to interview anybody happening by.

Dobrowski had said, "Egress?"

Nash said, "One way. Exit only."

"I got a vague idea what it means," Dobrowski said. "But I don't see any pretty teachers around you're trying to impress."

They went back inside, walked the length of each corridor, trying both side doors, Dobrowski pointing out there'd be no use fingerprinting the heavy doors or the brass crash bar. A thousand adolescents had passed through those doors in the last forty-eight hours. The east side door was a few feet closer to the main office, so the most likely exit, the killer coming out, looking left and right, going right, down the half flight of wide stairs, hitting the crash bar with his hip, out through the doors, and then just fifty yards or so to the parking lot.

A large dumpster was tucked at the side of the building just around the corner from the east exit. They were looking at it. Dobrowski was talking about some city schools in the States having metal detectors and a squad of security guards. Maybe it'll come to that up here. Nash said, "Think we need to go through it?"

Dobrowski saw he was looking at the dumpster. He said, "Leave it for the crime scene boys. They can go diving or take the whole thing home, whatever they want."

Back inside the outer office, the principal had arrived, looking crestfallen, distraught, sitting behind a desk, one hand kneading his forehead. He was telling a uniform cop about his school having the best safety record in the city. "It's a safe school," he was saying over and over. And then, this had to be an outsider, some gang member. Couldn't be one of his students. Nash wasn't sure if he was reassuring himself or preparing to meet the press.

The MO was straightening up, closing his bag, stripping off his latex gloves. Seeing Nash, he said, "She died fifteen, thirty minutes before being discovered. Multiple stab wounds to the chest and abdomen. Enough to say there was a little anger involved, not enough to make it especially personal. I'll have to take a closer look, but the wounds seem a little ragged."

"That means?"

"Your weapon was a knife, but maybe not very sharp, or serrated. Fairly big."

Dobrowski said, "Her purse is sitting on the desk untouched. Her computer's there. There'd be nothing else in here worth stealing. Unless she had a laptop." He was a big man, wide forehead, looked like an old football player, his coats always a little tight. He was frowning now, shaking his head. "What do we get? Six, eight homicides a year? But where they are, you know, it looks right. You expect it. Seedy hotel rooms, crack houses, the one in the Zanzibar last month. But not in a school. It shouldn't be happening here."

# Seven

Just inside the front door, she called, "I'm home."

Nobody answered. Sharon shed her coat, dropped her purse, headed straight for the bedrooms. She assumed Alicia would be glued to the screen on her Facebook, or TikTok, AirPods in her ears, homework spread out on the floor, cell alive and receiving a text message. Keeping in constant contact with friends and this new boy she mentioned in an offhand way, as if a break in their inane exchanges for more than ten minutes would send her hurtling alone and unloved into deep space. She remembered the evening a few months back Alicia had run into the kitchen saying, "Oh my God, oh my God," over and over, and Sharon had asked, "What's wrong, sweetie?" Then, panic in her eyes, Alicia had told her Snapchat was down, crashed in mid sentence, and her cell battery was dead.

She was, as Sharon had imagined, sitting at her desk, hands on the keyboard, a conversation about nothing scrolling down the screen, AirPods in place, papers and books scattered on the floor and bed, cell phone sitting beside the keyboard, receiving a text message. Sharon leaned over her, said directly into her right ear, "I'm home."

Alicia winced, closed the screen, said, "Do you have to shout?"

Sharon noticed she hadn't been startled, had probably listened to her from the driveway to her bedroom. She said, "Any word from Chris?"

Alicia picked up her cell. "He texted. He's not very good at it. I think he was asking if the coast was clear, like could he come home without getting into shit. I told him no problem, you'd already left for the hospital."

That had Sharon glancing at her watch, relieved her Christian was alive and in communication, and wanting to wring his neck. She said, "Shut everything off, sweetie, and come down to the living room. We need to have a little talk."

"We need to talk? It's your son who's not home, Mother."

"Not about that. Something else. And I only have an hour before going to work."

She had thought about calling in. It would be reasonable. She could claim acute PTSD. But what would she do all night besides watch old movies and worry? She opened a bottle of Aussie Shiraz, poured herself a good six ounces, stuffed the cork back in. She was aware the bottle had been gathering dust for a month now in the small rack on her kitchen counter. It was one of the problems or benefits of steady nights. Day shift, she'd have a glass of something in hand within minutes of coming in the door. But coming home from night shift meant drinking in the morning. She wasn't there yet. *But give it time*, she said to herself. *Give it time.*

When Alicia came down wearing that "What?" look on her face, Sharon was flipping through channels trying to find local news. She said, "Just watch this for a minute. It'll explain."

Alicia sprawled in the armchair, legs stretched out. She said,

"Mom, it's a documentary about pig farming. If you want me to clean my room, just say so. You don't have to be so circumspect." She said the last word as if she had just graduated from a school of elocution.

Sharon said, "No. The news. It's coming."

Alicia sat up when she saw the establishing shot of what they called "a local high school" aligned with the words "unfolding tragedy."

Afterward came the torrent of questions. "They didn't say which teacher. Is that why you were late? Oh my God. Oh my God. Who is it? You know, don't you, Mom?"

Sharon was about to tell her, thinking how much to tell her, when they heard a key in the front door, and then the door bang open against the wall, Christian, as usual, underestimating his strength, or maybe stoned or drunk. He walked past them, small pack on his shoulders, glancing their way and then, averting his eyes, heading straight for the half flight of stairs to the bedrooms. Not even stopping at the refrigerator. She called after him, got no response. Sitting with Alicia, she became aware of his size, always noticing this when she hadn't seen him for a day or two. Six foot three now, adolescent clumsy, sloppy, usually walking with a slight hunch, ball cap on, sometimes sideways.

She looked at her watch, found herself almost grateful she had to leave for work in a few minutes and could put the confrontation off another day. Alicia had watched her brother go by, and now she was looking at Sharon, her sharp little mind working overtime. God help her, Sharon had watched for bloodstains on his pants as he lurched by. She hadn't seen any.

She told Alicia to go to bed now. They'd deal with this in the morning. She could see Alicia was torn between trying to get more information from her mother and getting on her computer and cell to text the semaphore of the day, "OMG, OMG."

She said, "Go to bed. I'm sure there'll be no school tomorrow. We can talk when I get home."

Christian was in the bathroom. She knocked on the door loudly, heard the indignant "What?" from the other side, then the tap running. She told him, as firmly as she could muster, to get his sorry ass in bed and stay there. And be here in the morning when she gets home or she'll...She paused here. Then she said, "Or I'll simply lock you out of the goddamn house. You hear me?"

She couldn't make out what he said then, probably some profanity. She repeated, "Did you hear what I said?"

"Yeah. Whatever."

She let out a breath, knew "whatever" was probably the best she'd get from him, that adolescent way of acquiescing without giving up an inch of territory.

# Eight

His momma was bipolar, she told him herself. He had said, "No kidding. I thought you were just plain crazy." He had given her a big grin and watched her glare turn into a smile. He preferred her depressed, though, when she'd sit for hours watching televangelists, not care about what he did or didn't do, at least until she stopped getting out of bed and he'd have to call the nurse at the clinic. Mary was her name, the nurse who came when he called. Woman about the same age as his mother, nothing to look at, hefty, dressed in drab, but a liveliness in her eyes. She'd come some time the same day he called, talk to his mother in the bedroom that now smelled of old lady, then get on her cell to the doctor. Sometimes, they'd send an ambulance to get her. Sometimes, Mary would tell Jerome they had to mobilize her—that was her word, mobilize, like it was just a matter of turning on the ignition. Maybe she'd take a sample of blood, see if her chemicals needed adjusting. She'd show Jerome his momma's pills, tell him which is which and when she had to take them. Jerome always listening for the ones ended with "-pam" knowing those were the ones he might borrow now and then.

Mary would say, "She's missed a few of her lithium, I see, but used up all her lorazepam." She'd look at Jerome, eyes on him, not accusing him directly but looking like she knew where those lorazepam may have gone. Then she'd put all of his momma's pills in this dosette thingy, little boxes Monday through Sunday.

Just before she left, she'd always say something like, "Your mother's lucky to have you around to look after her, Jerome. You make sure she eats something now." Causing him enough guilt to keep his fingers out of her pill box for a few days. At least until he badly needed one of those pams to ease himself off some ludes.

Ah, but this morning, she was manic, what Mary called hypo-manic, which he didn't quite understand. He figured mania was those times you got to talk with God, wear robes and bells, and run down the street screaming about the second coming of Christ. Or like that short Eyetalian on C range, spent the day pacing and talking a fucking blue streak, wouldn't take no medication, until he collapsed in a heap and pissed himself, guards figuring someone clobbered him, but he'd just run out of gas. Still, it'd be more interesting than what his momma did when she was hypo-manic, which she was doing when he arrived home this morning: buying shit from the Shopper's Channel like it was a going-out-of-business sale, and filling out those Publishers Clearing House contest forms. The house was already full of this stuff—pissy little clock radios shaped like toy rockets, fake diamond rings, sets of sterling silver knives and forks didn't have enough silver on them to fill a tooth.

She was in her chair in front of the TV when he let himself in the front door, the TV loud with this blonde and a fairy taking turns pitching some junk, regular $250 now, this time only, $99.95, but wait, it also comes with a unique, but wait, not only that but our first hundred callers will receive...He thought, *God help us she ever discovers eBay.*

She had the telephone in her lap to be quick on the dial, leaning forward in her chair, not be number one hundred and one and miss out on that extra piece of plastic shit they were piling into the offer. Without so much as a hello, how ya doing, or taking her eyes off the TV case she missed a bargain, she said, "Jerome, is that you? Came in the mail this morning, right there on the table ready to go out. Says I've already won $37,000. I didn't even have to subscribe to anything, but I did anyway. I think it was one of those country life magazines. Will you be a dear and make sure it gets in the mailbox down at the corner, or better yet, you don't mind, take it to the little post office on King, back of the Shopper's Drug, make sure it gets in the right slot?"

He said, "Sure, Mom, right after I clean up a little, have a nap." The other trouble with these hypo-manic periods was she'd want to cook for him, and she was not a good cook. Then when she'd watched him eat, and treated herself to a little sherry, the little bit she called a drop of sherry, being more like half a bottle of the stuff he couldn't stand himself, she'd get this dreamy look in her eyes, and start talking about his brother and what a beautiful young man he'd be now if he'd lived.

Once he'd come home to find her sitting in her chair with the TV off, but talking to someone in the room wasn't there. Took him a few minutes to figure it was his little brother she was talking to. He'd called Mary and told her she was talking to her son, Justin. Mary had said, "Uh huh." Like she was waiting for more. And Jerome had said, "Did I neglect to mention that Justin is dead? Died in a swimming accident when he was just a kid." *Also in a lake and in his swimming trunks*, Jerome found himself thinking, his mind taking a trip to the absurd rather than think too much about baby brother Justin. "I'll be over in about an hour," Mary had told him. Main thing got her talking to the dead and departed, it turned out, was a second bottle of sherry, mixed with her pams.

At the foot of the stairs, he changed his mind and detoured to the kitchen to rummage through the refrigerator. She was on him quickly, leaning in over his shoulder, saying, "What would you like? Let me fix it for you."

There was no getting away from it now. He sat down at the kitchen table, said, "Sure, Mom. How about a grilled cheese?" There was nothing much she could do to ruin a grilled cheese. Unless she decided to experiment with some weird spice. Maybe he should get Mary on the phone, tell her his mother is trying to poison him, get her sent away for a while. Such were his reveries until, standing at the counter, buttering the bread on both sides for the frying pan, she said, "I almost forgot. Your PO called. The pretty one. Sam. Says you need to see her ten tomorrow morning."

Which meant a urine test. It reminded him why he tried the hospital scam: he tests positive he's got a doctor's note saying why a controlled substance was circulating in his veins. If it had worked, which it didn't, thanks to that cold bitch nurse. The bit of cannabis provided by Sal might still show, but everything else would be clear by then. He didn't think she'd breach him for a little THC lingering in his fat cells, or he could take in a sample of his mother's urine, but then all those pams would show up. He decided to eat his grilled cheese and worry about tomorrow tomorrow.

His mother put this oversize sandwich on a plate in front of him, melted cheddar spilling out the sides, ketchup bottle beside it. She said, "You must be hungry, up all night on that security job."

It was a second before he remembered he'd hinted, well, maybe he told her, that's what he'd be doing, nighttime security at a factory downtown, the one makes mustard. She wasn't dumb, though. Had probably figured nobody would give a security job to a convicted felon. But you know mommas, always wanting to think the best of their little boys, ready to believe anything they say. "Yeah," he said. "Not much to it 'cept you gotta keep awake."

"They give you a uniform?" she asked.

"Uh huh," said through a mouthful of sandwich dipped in ketchup. Nothing else added this time, thank Christ. "You leave it in a locker there. Don't have to bring it home."

He knew this really didn't make too much sense, but she was easily distracted. He said, "So how much you think you won?"

She said, "Right. Thirty-seven thousand dollars. They'll be coming to my door just like those TV ads, if you remember to mail that letter. It says that's all I've gotta do. Would you like another one? No? Well, you eat up now, and I think I might just celebrate my good fortune."

He saw she was reaching for the bottle of sherry in the same cupboard she kept Windex and detergents, above the vacuum cleaner. He said, "A little early for that, isn't it, Mom?"

She said, "I do believe the sun is past the yardarm."

He said, "What the fuck is a yardarm?" She was pouring herself a large glass and seemed distracted, so he decided to leave well enough alone, take a little nap. After all, he'd been up all night preventing bad guys from stealing the mustard. And he'd have to stay clean tonight. He was going to visit his PO tomorrow, but maybe he could at least get laid. On his way up the stairs, he shouted back to her, "Would you turn that fucking TV down for a few hours? Can you do that?" He didn't wait for an answer.

# Nine

"Where were you last night?"

"I was in bed. Asleep."

Sharon said, "No. You know what I mean. The night before last night. You didn't come home at all."

Her shift had been quiet. No one had caught the local news, and she didn't feel like getting into it, telling them about her visit to the school, finding a body. And she surmised the body in question had not been brought to the emergency that evening, or there would have been a buzz about it. Straight to the morgue, she guessed, to await autopsy. At one point between ambulances, Zabodny had told her she looked preoccupied, sitting in the small lounge, staring into space. She had brushed him off with a slight smile. He had said, "Let me buy you a coffee." And filled a mug with brown liquid from the urn.

She told him, "Remember, you owe me a real coffee." But there was the problem of having a fling with a younger man standing right in front of her. What would they talk about? All that was on her mind at the moment was her seventeen-year-old son. She couldn't talk to Zabodny about him. He wouldn't be interested, and even if he were, what's he going to say? Besides, she tells him she has two teenagers at home, it would probably scare him half to death. She settled for asking him if he had any children.

"Not even married," he said. Then, "You got problems with yours?"

She was almost going to tell him, pulled herself back, and said instead, "Why aren't you married?" Then the ambulance arrived, the one they'd been called about twenty minutes ago, bringing an old woman from a nursing home, bleeding from both ends. Zabodny hadn't answered. Getting up, he said, trying to make it sound like he had ten more years' experience than he actually had, "They need to lock up the Aspirin in those places."

Now she was home, and had discovered, to her surprise, that Christian was already up out of bed, showered and dressed and sitting at the kitchen table eating a bowl of Captain Crunch, the morning newspaper spread out beside his glass of orange juice. Alicia was still in the bathroom.

"The night before?" he asked, like it would really stretch his memory to go back that far.

"Yes. The night before last."

"You see this?" he said, tilting his head toward the headlines.

She glanced at the newspaper and saw the big print lead, "Teacher Murdered."

He said, "It doesn't say who it is."

She said, "Do you know anything about it, Christian?"

"What? Why would I know anything?"

"That's right. I forgot. You don't even go to that school."

"Yes, I do. What are you talking about?"

"Not very often, according to Ms. Darnell."

"Darnell, the VP? She's an idiot."

"Christian?"

"You know what I mean. I haven't skipped that much."

Alicia had just entered the kitchen. She said, "Ms. Darnell? Is she the one, like I mean, is she?"

Sharon said, "Yes. She's the one."

Alicia said, "Oh. It makes me feel creepy all over." She sat down. "Oh my God. Oh my God."

Christian stared dumbly. Then he said, "How do you know it's Darnell? They take her to the hospital?"

"No," said Sharon, sitting down at the table. "I was the one who found her."

"No shit. Really?"

"Yes, really."

"But, I mean, what were you doing there?"

"It's back to my first question, Christian. I was meeting with her to talk about your truancy."

Alicia said, "That must have been horrible. I mean, finding her body."

"It was."

Christian said, "Do they know who did it?"

Not really wanting to go there, Sharon gave her son a long, hard look. "Have you had any dealings with her, Christian?"

He said, "What? No. She was my homeroom last year. I think she just does administration this year. I didn't mean she's an idiot."

"She would deal with truancy, wouldn't she?"

"I guess."

"Did she talk to you about skipping?"

"No. I swear to God. I haven't skipped that much. Really."

"And you still haven't told me where you were the night before last."

Christian's eyes were on the table, his head lowered. He said, "I lost track of time playing *World of Warcraft* with Jaimie. So I just crashed. You were at the hospital, so there was no way of getting hold of you."

She sighed, thinking, *That's why I carry a cell and leave it on in my locker*. But she let it go. "And after that? Yesterday."

"That's a different story."

"I'm all ears."

Alicia had turned away from the table. By the hunch of her shoulders, Sharon could tell she was texting like mad. Undoubtedly telegraphing her inside information to the world: "OMG, OMG, it's Darnell."

She swung around and said, "We're going to be late."

Sharon said, "This would be one day I'd be happy if you both stayed home."

"No way, Mom. There'll be special assemblies, and the crisis team'll be there. And Becky. I have to see Becky. Ms. Darnell helped her through her parents' divorce. She'll be just devastated. I mean, like really messed up."

They had left for school, brother and sister, walking to the corner to catch the city bus that would take them to the front door of Pearson Secondary. As it should be, as if nothing were wrong. Christian looking after his little sister, he being in grade eleven, she in nine, a little ahead of her age, having been advanced one year, he probably doing a mix of grade ten and eleven classes. She could never get a straight answer out of him. Only those tried and true evasive techniques: "Pretty much," "Mostly," "Basically," and "Sure, yeah, of course. What do you think I'm a dummy?"

As always, at the door, Christian towering over her, she had asked herself how on earth this had happened, her baby boy becoming a giant, though she knew six foot three was no longer unusual. Alicia had asked for bus fare and lunch money. Christian hadn't. She didn't think of this oddity until they were gone. His eyes looked clear this morning. He hadn't been especially surly. At least this once, he had passed her perfunctory cannabis inspection. He was neither high nor in withdrawal. She also knew amphetamines and OxyContin were harder to detect. As they walked away from the house, she could imagine Alicia talking and talking, Christian trying to work out in his mind how to be cool about Darnell's death without appearing callous. Although callous certainly wouldn't be his word. Wanting to appear cool but not...what? Maybe cool but not cold. She had heard him use that word, as in, "That's just cold." When she was giving him some well-deserved reprimand. Or, for that matter, telling them about some obnoxious drunk she had kicked out of the emergency.

As she pulled the blinds and turned on her fan, she decided to believe all was well. Her children were just fine, thank you very much. Normal twenty-first-century teenagers. As in very confused, entitled, insufferable, but probably turning out okay, eventually. Hamish would take them this weekend, and, after doing some shopping, cleaning the house, she'd have a few hours for herself. To do what exactly? Let's face it, she told herself just before nodding off, her mother would call.

# Ten

Nash and Dobrowski were at the school by 8:30, pulling in just ahead of a CHCH mobile unit, undoubtedly hoping for some student reaction shots, maybe already planning an extended piece on school safety. Ms. Darnell's office was taped off, but the principal, who looked, as Dobrowski had mentioned to Nash yesterday, just like a principal should, had gathered the support staff in the outer office to brief them. "The spitting image of Principal Conklin," Dobrowski had said.

"Who?" Nash asked. "Guy from *Happy Days*?"

"No. Way before that. Remember Miss Brooks?"

Nash had said, "No. I don't remember Miss Brooks, but then you're a lot older than I am. Come to think of it, how would you know what a radio show high school principal looked like?"

Dobrowski was thinking there had to have been a television version for this clear image in his mind, especially the bald head and the monk's fringe, but his interest in the question lagged. He said, "Who would want to kill a teacher?"

Nash had answered, "Probably a minimum five students from each class she's taught."

As the students arrived, they were all directed to the auditorium for a special assembly. About half came to school, the rest kept home after their parents had read the morning newspaper or seen the ten o'clock news the night before. Dobrowski stayed in the principal's office, learning what he could about Ms. Darnell from the secretaries. Nash wandered along the empty corridor once the students had all been herded into the auditorium. They had asked the principal to include, in his talk to the students, an invitation for any student who might know some pertinent information to please visit the office to talk to one of the investigating detectives. They didn't expect anyone to come forward. They knew teenagers stuck with the code of silence better than your average drug cartel.

On the main floor, Nash walked past the boys' washroom. He stopped. He shrugged to himself, entered quickly, and rounded the corner in time to catch a boy standing by the sinks, hiding his right hand behind his back. Another boy was standing there too, facing away from the sinks. Maybe sixteen, seventeen. The taller of the two with the forbidden cigarette or joint behind his back had gelled hair, spiked in the centre, one earring, eyebrow ring, low baggy pants. The other was pudgy, nervous.

Nash said, "Hey, hey. We gonna share that or what?"

They both looked startled. The boy with an eyebrow ring quickly pulled himself together, calling up the best attitude he could muster, that look of disdain and dismissal. He said, "What's it to you, dude?"

Nash wanted to slap the little fuck, or at least let his coat fall open to reveal his holster, but instead he sighed and gave the kid a long, hard look. He said, "You heard me. Let's see what you've got in your right hand."

The boy shrugged. Without giving up the look on his face, he showed Nash the stub of a joint. Nash took it, held it to his nose to sniff. He said, "I'm relieved. For a minute there, I thought you boys were using something could be dangerous to your health."

The chubby one screwed up his face, looked puzzled.

Nash said, "I mean like tobacco, Marlboro, Player's Light. But this here weed is a natural hand-rolled product." He handed the roach back to the boy. "Am I right?"

The kid said, "Yeah, sure. If you say so."

"What I do say," said Nash, turning to the closest urinal and unzipping, "is that I will forget about the controlled substance you two young men are misusing in the boys' washroom, if you tell me all you know about Ms. Darnell."

"We don't know nothing," offered the boy with the roach.

As Nash finished and zipped up and then turned to the boys, he said, "I know you don't know nothing. You're teenage boys. Ad-do-less-cents. By definition, you know nothing, less than nothing, in fact. Sweet dick all is what you know in the great scheme of things. But what I want to know from you is what you think of Ms. Darnell. Anybody you can think of not like her that much?"

The chubby one said, "I had her last year. She wasn't so bad. Tough, though."

"C'mon, you can do better than that. You want your daddies to know you were kicked out of school on account of smoking marijuana in the washroom?"

The skinny one said, "She's got a thing about drugs, though."

"Had a thing about drugs."

"Yeah, right. Like it was a religion. She thought every second kid in the school was high on something."

The chubby one muttered, "She could be right."

Nash said, "Yeah, and what was she doing about it?"

"She'd talk about it a lot, you know, at assembly. And if she thought you were bad into it, she'd call in your parents. She'd rat you out."

Nash said, "Uh huh. Any particular kid in her bad books?"

The skinny one said, "No, man. That's all I know."

"What about a kid called Christian Gibson? You know him?"

"Yeah, we know him," said the fat kid.

The taller one gave him a look.

When the telephone woke her at 11:30, she realized she had left it on this time, some premonition causing her to do this. Usually, she turned the ringer off on the landline, leaving her cell for emergencies—only her kids, close friends, her mother, and the hospital knowing her cell number, all of whom also knew she worked night shift, and needed at least six goddamn hours of sleep during the day. She hoped it was someone selling something, one of those "Mrs. Gibson, are you fully satisfied with your current provider?" questions. She would love to tell them just how satisfied she was being so rudely disturbed after a night shift at the trauma centre.

But the voice was a man's, somewhat familiar, saying, "Mrs. Gibson, this is Detective Nash."

All she could muster in response was a rising cadence, "Yes?"

"We were going to come out and have a talk with you, just seeing if you're home."

"I work nights, you know. I was asleep when the phone rang."

"Well, that's really why I called. Thought we'd warn you about visiting."

She said, "It can't wait?"

"No," said Nash.

They arrived in an unmarked car, Nash and his partner, the big one. The big one looking like an old football player shoehorned into a suit, shaved head. Nash a little smaller, full head of dark, maybe black hair, cut short, smart eyes. Sharon watched them approach the house, unmistakably two detectives on official business. She had showered and made coffee and waited for their arrival at one o'clock. Nash had not been willing to discuss anything on the phone.

When she opened the door, Nash asked if they could come in to talk comfortably. He was half in, his partner looking over his shoulder, before she said, "Sure, why not? Would either of you like a coffee?"

They sat in the living room, suits and ties, large shoes, the requisite overcoats, the ones they must sell in special detective stores. Both of them big men looking out of place in her small house. She brought them each a mug of coffee on a tray with milk and sugar. She could see that Nash had been up looking at photos on the wall and one end table when she returned from the kitchen. She said, "Okay. Let's get on with it so I can get back to bed. I assume you want to know if I can remember anything else."

Nash said, "Not exactly. We found Ms. Darnell's appointment book, at least the electronic version on her computer, along with notes about appointments."

He paused. Sharon didn't say anything. "Her appointment list says she was expecting to see you and your son, Christian."

"It says that? Me and Christian?"

"Well, actually she wrote 'Mrs. Gibson slash Christian.'"

"I can tell you he was not there with me, and 'Mrs. Gibson slash Christian' is ambiguous. She may have been referencing the particular student, that's all."

"There was more. Her notation about the meeting read..." Here, he pulled out his small notepad and appeared to look at it, all for effect, Sharon suspected. "Re: Christian's frequent absences and possible drug use."

Sharon said, "She didn't mention anything about drug use on the phone."

"But you suspected, I'm sure."

"Yes. Of course. He's seventeen. Aren't they all using pot these days?"

It was Dobrowski who spoke then. He said, "Not my kid. I catch him at it, he's dead."

Sharon said, "It's easy to say that. Much harder to deal with when it happens."

Nash said, "And where would Christian be now?"

Sharon responded quickly, "He's at school."

"Well, no, actually. We were just there. No Christian Gibson to be found."

"Then I have no idea where he is. Probably playing hooky with one of his buddies."

Nash took a swallow of his coffee. "You mind if we take a look in his room?"

"He's not home, I told you. I'm not going to lie about that?"

"All the same," said Nash, "we need to look for ourselves."

Sharon hesitated, decided there was no point getting defensive. She said, "Okay. Suit yourself. It's the last door on the upper level. You can't miss it. And while you're there, you mind cleaning up, picking the clothes off the floor, bringing down the garbage?"

Dobrowski said, "They tell me teenage girls are worse. I wouldn't know. I've only got a boy. The one I mentioned before. Now and then, we run out of glasses and plates. We know where to look, his mother and me."

Sharon figured he was simply holding her with conversation, giving Detective Harry Nash some time without her watching him tear the place apart. She wondered what Dobrowski's first name was. She did her best to stay calm, spooned another sugar in her coffee, decided she'd think of them as Harry and Bigfoot. Harry could go to town in Christian's room; he couldn't possibly make it look worse. This made her think of a joke: How can you tell a teenager's room from a room tossed by two cops? She realized her anxiety was getting the better of her, but she couldn't stop the thought. There are no half-eaten donuts in the tossed room. Or maybe it would work the other way around. You can find half-eaten donuts in the teenager's room. She focused on her coffee cup, added more sugar.

Dobrowski saw she wasn't moving and joined his partner.

When they returned, they didn't sit. Nash said, "Well, the good news is we didn't find any food more than six months old, and no drugs or drug paraphernalia. But you know if your son is one to save up his allowance, Mrs. Gibson?"

Sharon said, "You're asking because?"

"Quite a wad of cash he's got stashed in his sweater drawer."

"What is 'quite a wad of cash'?"

"Close to four thousand dollars."

"You've got to be kidding." She was doing some quick math in her head, adding up Christmas and birthday money from his grandparents, from his father, but she knew it would come in about 3,900 short.

Sharon sighed, sat back in her chair. They didn't sit this time.

"I think maybe we should have a talk with him when he gets home, Mrs. Gibson. You think you could give us a call, maybe, Mrs. Gibson, when he gets home, I mean, or bring him down to the station?"

"What? Sorry. I mean, is that the thing..." She lost track of her thought.

Nash said, "Here's a card with a direct line to my desk. You'll call when he gets home? Right? Don't ask him about the money. Just give us a call, alright?" He turned toward the door, Dobrowski already there waiting for him. Then, as if having an afterthought, Nash turned back to Sharon, pulled a photograph from his pocket, showed it to her.

It looked to Sharon like a twelve-inch ruler lying on a table, and next to that, a knife of some sort about the same length with a heavy-looking handle. Not a kitchen knife.

Nash said, "Does Christian own anything like this, Mrs. Gibson?"

She stared at the photo. Her mouth was dry. She shook her head. Her impulse was to talk. To talk rapidly, explain how he was a boy—of course he owned knives, didn't all boys? Fishing knives, hunting knives. She quelled that impulse and simply shook her head without making eye contact. Then she said, "Is that really what you were looking for in his room?"

Nash said, "No, Mrs. Gibson. We already have the knife. We're looking for the owner."

They didn't wait for a response, and Sharon, though thinking rapidly, couldn't give them one.

# Eleven

Jerome pushed the button beside the intercom.

His appointment with his PO had been uneventful. He had peed in a cup; she had asked him a few questions, mostly about looking for work. She did say, "I hope you're taking good care of your mother. She's been through a lot." He told her he was making sure she had enough to eat, helping with the laundry, couldn't keep her from buying shit off that Shoppers' Channel, though, or nipping on the sherry.

It had been a bummer of a night. He had to keep sober for his appointment this morning, and he was just no good picking up women cold sober. Became a kid again, stammering some bullshit, trying to cover up the fact he was just interested in getting laid, period. And sitting there trying to look deep and mysterious and a little dangerous while sipping a Coca-Cola didn't cut it either. Only ones sat beside him were the pros and he sure as hell wasn't ready to pay for it. He had said to one of them, "Do I look desperate to you?" And the whore had said, "Now that you mention it, honey." That's when he got up and left, went home to his bed above his crazy mother.

But it gave him time to think about Sal, wondering if he was looking him up because he was a little gun-shy about trying something on his own after the last shit-fest. He'd play it cool, not show his hand, wait and see what Sal was up to, see if there was any real money in it, then he'd make him an offer he couldn't refuse.

Sal's voice came over the intercom. "Yes."

Jerome said, "It's Jerome."

The voice said, "State your business." Like he was some sort of *el jefe*.

"My business is your business," said Jerome.

"Come to apartment one oh seven."

"That's not the same one. Yesterday you were two oh seven."

"One oh seven. I see you alone, I open the door, I may not."

The lock buzzed open before Jerome had time to reply. He went in, walked past the elevator and looked for apartment 107 on the main floor.

It was another nondescript door except for the large fisheye at about the five-foot level. Jerome thought he heard at least three deadbolts slide before the door opened. He stepped in and Sal locked the door behind him.

Sal was looking him over, a little smile on his face. He said, "You visit me twice in two days. Do I owe you money?"

Jerome said, "No, man. Not yet. Yesterday, you lived one flight up."

"Ah. This is my office. It is not good to do business from your home."

Jerome took a kitchen chair, straddled it, noticed the crack pipes lying on the table, loaded and ready. He said, "You expecting a party?"

Sal sat down on the second chair. He said, "No, man. But I

think I will tell you. I am like Dell computer. Direct to the end user. The kids. They come to the door, give me five dollars, I let them have one deep pull, maybe two for a repeat customer. They want a third pull, another five bucks."

Jerome raised his eyebrows.

Sal explained, "I never open the door. It is all through the hole. I don't deal with crazy teenagers get bright ideas. If the kid looks a little old, maybe undercover, I say I don't know what the fuck he's talking about and close the hole, what you people call it, the fisheye. Then the cops don't get no probable cause to break down my door. If they come I'm not here, they got nothing on me. I live one flight up."

"Doesn't sound like a way to get rich."

"It is good, but tedious. Sometime two hundred bucks in an hour, but my hand cramps up."

Jerome said, "Maybe you could apply for Workers' Compensation."

"You make a joke. But maybe I do better if I have an outside sales force."

Jerome said, "This is a pretty small operation."

"I must keep a low profile for the next fourteen months."

"Yeah? Who's your PO?"

Sal didn't answer. He said, "You kill anyone besides your poppa?"

Jerome wanted to talk about it. He wanted to tell Sal, yeah, sure. Or maybe use that line from some movie, "Only the ones needed killing." But he held his tongue, figured he didn't want Sal to have anything on him, cagey bastard.

Sal said, "I see in your eyes, but you don't want to tell me. Is all right. Do you know how to cook?"

Jerome said, "Are we talking bacon and eggs or powder and soda?"

As she dialled, Sharon was thinking, *So much for a day to myself.* When Hamish came on the line, she said, "I thought you'd want to know the cops were here, and they found four thousand dollars in your son's bedroom." She had gone to check on it herself, carefully counted it, and put it back. Three thousand nine hundred and sixty dollars, to be exact. Then she had sat on Christian's bed for a good twenty minutes, looking around at the mess on the floor, the posters on the wall, wondering where that little boy of hers had gone. The little kid who was once scared of bats and thunderstorms.

"What?"

"Four thousand dollars."

"What were they doing in his bedroom?"

"They came to talk to me about that teacher's death. I was the one found the body."

"You found the body."

"Remember. I called you on the way to an appointment with the VP? That's the one. Killed in her office."

"You found her."

"Almost tripped on her."

He was silent for a moment, taking this in. She figured he'd be scrolling through some sympathetic comments, looking for one that wouldn't come across condescending, knowing how she'd react to that.

Then he said, "What were the cops doing in Christian's bedroom?"

"Looking for Christian."

"You let them in his bedroom? They need a warrant for that."

"I didn't...never mind. The point is your son has four thousand dollars in his sweater drawer."

"Maybe he's saved up. Or sold his PlayStation."

"It won't add up to four thousand, Hamish. And they want to talk with him."

"Jesus Christ."

There was a period of silence on the line. Sharon said, "Well? What do we do now?"

"I don't know, Sharon. I've never been involved in anything like this before."

Maybe it was just a statement of fact, but Sharon heard the unspoken, "Not in my family, at least." She hung up on him then, sure he was making reference to her older brother, living on a disability pension and drinking cheap liquor in some shack near Sudbury. A brother she hadn't spoken to in three years, not since that last Christmas visit when he'd stayed sober for all of twenty-four hours. But maybe Hamish just felt out of his league here. She picked up when he phoned back.

"You hung up on me."

"I'm sorry. I had a call coming in. I thought it might be Chris."

"You said they want to talk with him. You mean about the money they found?"

"No. I think about the teacher, the VP."

"The teacher?"

"And there's something else."

"What else could there possibly be?"

"I'll be there in an hour or so. We need to talk."

"We are talking."

"I mean properly, face to face. I need time to think."

"When?"

"I'll be there in an hour."

He began to mutter something about his busy day, his appointments, but she hung up again, and this time didn't pick up when her phone rang a few seconds later.

Sal said, "We're not living together, man. I'm asking, can you cook up a little rock?"

Jerome said, "I've watched it done. It's not complicated. Just gotta watch you don't burn some, turn it into tar. Have some patience."

"What else can you do?"

Jerome said, "I'm not interviewing for a job."

"No?"

"I figure we hang out together, see how it goes. See we got what they call complementary skill sets."

"Why I asked can you cook."

"Yeah, but that's women's work?" It almost came out *niggers' work*, but he caught himself. You never knew if these Hispanics were gonna laugh or knife you, you use the n-word.

Sal said, "When we expand, maybe. For now, I need someone cooking, watching my back, doing a little selling."

"Anything besides crack?"

"You can make crystal?"

"You got the equipment?"

"Too dangerous. But we can sell a little."

Jerome said, "You're renting two apartments in the same building."

"I esplained."

"Your landlord's not curious?"

Sal tilted his head, looked pained, but before he could speak, the intercom buzzed. He held the button and answered. Jerome could hear a young voice squeezed through a tiny speaker. Sal said to Jerome, "Here, I show you how it's done. Watch through the fisheye."

Jerome bent awkwardly to watch. With the lens in place, he could see the whole corridor. Two young guys were walking nervously toward the door of the apartment.

Sal said, "What do you see?"

"Two kids, maybe fifteen, sixteen."

"Not old enough to be undercover?"

"Just two fucking kids."

"Okay, they get to the door, you slide the lens back, they give you money."

"Yeah?" He could see them standing at the door, nervously shifting from foot to foot.

Jerome fumbled with the fisheye, found that it slid open on a tiny screw. A rolled five-dollar bill appeared through the hole. He took it. Sal came over with a long glass pipe, the business end covered in mesh with a small white rock sitting on top. He pushed the stem through the hole, lit a flame with his lighter, held the flame to the rock. The stem was bumping up and down. Sal said at the door, "Relax. Wait for it." The rock began to sizzle and smoke, and then cracked like a match. And the kid on the other end took a deep drag. And then another deep drag. Sal pulled the pipe back and let the fisheye lens cover the hole. He said, "You keep the five. I feel generous."

Jerome said, "I don't get it. Why not open the door, just sell the kid the rock?"

Sal said, "You see this. The rock is still good. These kids can't afford a whole piece, and this way, I get much more for it. Maybe ten times. And the other thing, the kid's wired or something, nobody can hear or see anything. And what I may or may not have sold the kid is gone. Poof. Very difficult for the cops to prove anything happened here. Very difficult. And the kid. He doesn't have anything on him the cops stop him or his momma checks his pockets."

Jerome said, "But the whole thing comes close to being work, man. Like serving coffee at Tims."

Sal said, "Pays a little better."

Nash was saying, "Who would have thought they'd have a team in the NHL called the Mighty Ducks? You think the Rocket would have guessed that?" He sipped from a hole in the top of his Tim Hortons large. "Not only that, these Mighty Ducks skating all over *Les Habitants*, you believe it?" He didn't wait for an answer, went on with his rant. "And then that little peckerhead has a hard-on for Hamilton. No team, no way. Even though it'd be the second-largest revenue source in the league. This is a hockey town, no doubt about it. And they'd pull from Cambridge, Brantford, Kitchener. Thing I don't understand. From a business sense, it makes sense, and these guys are businessmen. Right? And businessmen don't give a shit about anything but the bottom line. Right? No. Fucking schoolgirls is what they are. You didn't ask politely, Mr. Baldesini. Oh my! Oh my! My feelings are hurt. So fuck you."

Dobrowski had finished his coffee, a large double double, and was rolling up the rim with his front teeth. He read the rim, "'Play again.' You know, on the sports book, I could of won six hundred last night I didn't listen to you."

Nash said, "You never win."

They were sitting in an unmarked car opposite the Video Palace, waiting, seeing who was going in and out. They figured on picking up young Christian Gibson on his way out, probably holding a baggy or two, so they could keep him a while. Dobrowski put his empty cup in the holder between them. He said, "I got the other four winners and then I picked Montreal over Anaheim, on your advice. Did I mention 'on your advice'?"

"Close only counts in horseshoes," said Nash, looking across the street at the entrance.

"You're not going to take responsibility for my loss?"

"Like I say, you always lose."

"Bullshit. I'm two thousand up so far this year."

"You keep track of it?"

"Absolutely. Gamblers lie to themselves. All the time. So I write it down, look at it every week. I got it on a spreadsheet."

"Beth make you do that?"

"How'd you guess?"

Nash drank the last of his coffee, said, "He could be in there all day, and I'm gonna have to piss. Let me go flush him out."

"We've got nothing to hold him."

Nash was getting out of the car. He said, "Chances are he'll run. Pull the unit into the alley over there."

He walked across the street, dodging the light mid-afternoon traffic, and entered the double glass doors of the Video Palace. He could see only a handful of kids, teens, boys, on the games. A few years back, the place would be packed, the latest games drawing crowds. Now most of these kids have access in Mommy and Daddy's basement. He turned toward a washroom just inside the door and heard a voice say, "Customers only, buddy."

Nash glanced at the back of the store and then at the baseball caps and hoodies hunkered over consoles. He gave the guy who had spoken a cold look, a scruffy-looking twenty-something behind a counter. When he came out, the guy was sitting on a stool, avoiding eye contact. Nash walked toward the back, threading his way between machines. A dozen boys were sitting and standing at consoles, shooting up a storm. All wearing the same uniform: baseball cap on sideways, hair spilling out, baggy jackets, jeans with the crotch around the knees, dangling chains on the side, some with hoodies over the ball cap. He stood there a moment, wondering if they'd notice a big cop standing over them, mesmerized by the dazzling action on their little screens. Then he said, loudly, "I'm looking for Christian Gibson."

Only a couple of them pulled their eyes from the screens, and one quickly averted his, and then stooped low, trying to hide his big shoulders, and then made a clumsy run for the side door.

Nash said, "Goddammit." And broke into a run behind the kid, who was now going through the crash bars to the back alley.

When Nash emerged into the alley and the bright spring sunlight, the kid was already in the position, hands outstretched, face against the side of the building, Dobrowski patting him down.

They put him in the back seat of their car, the doors locking, and got in the front, Dobrowski behind the wheel.

Nash said, "They always run, y'know that. They always run. They holding, not holding. It doesn't matter. They always fucking run."

# Twelve

Sal said, "What I want to know if you're a lifer."

Jerome thought the little fuck who had to stand on tiptoe to look over a counter was full of himself. He said, "What I see here is you got nothing. It's nigger's work selling to children." He used the n-word this time, wanted to see what Sal did with it.

The n-word didn't seem to phase Sal. He looked at Jerome in that way of his, said, "I tole you. Keep a low profile for now. Don't attract the bikers. Build a little capital, but I think you don't last long. You have the attention span of a mariposa."

Jerome was wondering what a Mexican band had to do with anything when Sal added, "You do anybody besides your old man?"

"Maybe there was another," said Jerome.

They were sitting at the kitchen table of Sal's working apartment, Jerome's eyes drifting toward the small foil-wrapped rocks. But he was trying hard to be smart this time, be a seller, not a user. He would play along with this little greaser, not give him too much.

Sal said, "But you are not a natural-born killer, I think."

Jerome said, "What? You think it's something you inherit?" His old man had done ten years for manslaughter, but the way he heard the story was he was full of PCP at the time, nothing natural about it. "I figure it's something you grow into. Number three should be easy."

He tried to let Sal know with his eyes just who might become number three, but Sal grinned and said, "Okay, I think you might be useful. So, today, I let you have half. What the gringos call a gesture of good will."

Jerome knew he was referring to the pile of fives he had sorted into bundles of 200. He wanted to be sitting somewhere the cocaine came in plastic baggies inside designer luggage and the bundles of bills were 100s sorted into piles of 10,000. He could hear his momma saying, "If wishes were horses, beggars would ride." Whatever the hell that meant. He was thinking his momma's advice needed a serious update as he grabbed a bundle before Sal changed his mind.

In his Honda Civic, heading down Upper Wentworth, Jerome thought of something else his mother might say about now. That his money was burning a hole in his pocket. Damned if it wasn't true, the wad of bills stuck in his right front feeling good against his thigh, sort of warm and begging him to risk a positive urine and a breech.

At the very least, his PO would send him back to NA, and that would be shit, every Tuesday afternoon having to tell some group of losers, "Hi, my name is Jerome, and I was addicted to crystal meth," and some gangbanger would say back to him, "You are addicted man, not was addicted. Once addicted, always addicted. You're an addict in recovery, man." Sure, whatever. And someone else would say, "Good for you, Jerome. Hi, Jerome." Course, a few of them would be holding and one or two would be selling so there could be some value to it.

Before he came to the cut to Lower East Hamilton, the route down what the locals called the mountain, he had decided to use part of the 200 to buy himself a membership at Gold's, get some muscle on himself while he waited to see Sal's play, decide whether to rip the little shit or partner with him. The greaser always asking him about who he killed besides his daddy, trying to get something on him.

Not that he was proud of shooting the Jamaican, but maybe proud he was able to do it the time came, the necessity. Though he wondered if he'd of done it if he hadn't been tripping. He decided, yeah, same circumstances he'd have to. The fucker's own fault. He'd been out of the house like Arlene had told him, he'd still be alive, unless the bikers caught up to him dealing in their territory. The fucker had a death wish anyway, setting up shop with no backing. But they never got him for it. Cops always following the easy trail, assumed the bikers got him, burned the place down. Same smart-ass group had bought back their clubhouse.

"That's a hoot," his momma had said, reading the paper a few years ago. "Downtown, the Hell's Angels have this clubhouse, you know—steel door, bars, the works, got seized along with drugs and guns, the proceedings of crime—and they wait till the property comes up for public auction a year later and buy it back. What a hoot."

Jerome wasn't sure the wording was "proceedings of crime," but otherwise, she was right. Although irony might be a better word than hoot. Not that he'd ever understood the fucking word irony, but the bikers buying their clubhouse back at auction was fucking A for sure. He'd of loved to see the faces of the cops who did the bust in the first place. He wondered if they were still using it, or had bought the place back just to make a point. Fucking A. Maybe it was four years ago, before he looked up his old cellmate Albert and got himself in the last shit-fest, Albert trying his best to stay clean at the time.

He hadn't thought about Arlene and that peckerhead Albert for a couple of years. Maybe he should look them up, see if Arlene was still hot and putting out for a small piece of rock. Not likely if she's hooked. Probably got that squeezed-mouth rotten-teeth thing going, scabs all over her face, hepatitis, all that shit. The men on crack, they just go thin and stupid. The women get coyote ugly, still trying to offer up a little pussy in exchange for a few minutes of feeling like a girl again.

*Least*, he thought, feeling the wad of cash in his jeans, *if I have to pay for it tonight I can buy something clean and looks good.*

# Thirteen

Dobrowski had been part of the team investigating the killing of the lady lawyer and her husband up in the tony part of town. They'd known who was good for it from the first day—only ones with real motive and gravel for brains—a whole family of lowlifes who used a washed-up pro wrestler for muscle, liked to show his Glock in the bars of Hess Village when his pecs weren't doing it for him. One Johnny K-9. Cute.

But they'd gotten ahead of themselves, leaked a story to the press, said they'd obtained a confession from a jailhouse rat, implicating the family for a little consideration. It worked against the Musitanos, so why not against these lunkheads? They figured on turning them inward looking, so to speak. Instead, the city got handed a $2 million lawsuit, defamation of fucking character, if you can believe it, after the Crown attorney decided there just wasn't enough evidence to proceed. Which was why Detective Dobrowki was now reduced to babysitting teenagers. Don't you love this country? These guys slip away from the murder rap but now doing five years in a federal pen after the Mounties found them sharing a small fishing boat with a load of cocaine off the coast of Nova Scotia, and the city still has to defend itself against the lawsuit. Defamation of fucking character. The only one so far had to pay for the double homicide was Detective Dobrowski.

They were probably still running their crew from the pen and they'd be back in the city after two and a half years, double time before sentence plus good behaviour. Maybe in time to testify at discovery how their reputations had been besmirched irreparably by the murder accusation. Maybe they'd settle for half a mill and pay off the mortgage on their Ancaster house, or the one they had in Puerto Vallarta. Once they're back, he'd have to ask them why they did the husband along with the lady lawyer—he just happen to be there or was something else going on? Maybe the guy they hired just liked doing it, gave them a twosy for the price of one.

Nash was driving now. He'd put himself in the driver's seat while Dobrowski was stuffing young Christian in the back seat. The kid wasn't holding any baggies, so Nash just pointed the car east out Main Street, then down to the industrial district on Sherman, to park for a little while next to an abandoned factory. He figured there's no place as lonely and hopeless as an abandoned factory. Might soften the kid up without them touching him. They sat there for a few minutes in a lot next to the empty loading dock, doing nothing, saying nothing, looking out on the mottled asphalt where garbage and scrubby grasses competed in a silent reclamation project.

Christian managed a good front for half of that time, but when Dobrowski turned to look at him through the wire, he could see the little bastard was close to tears. Over six feet, but just a kid. He turned back and said to Nash, "You think we should work him over or just dump him in jail?" The kid starting to whimper.

Nash said, "Tell him he has the right to remain silent."

It was closer to two hours later when Sharon parked in a city lot next to the old house Hamish used for offices. Hamish Gibson, Insurance. She knew he had some kind of association with a couple of other brokers in the same building, passed clients around, shared a secretary. Sharon hadn't met this one, but she assumed she'd be blonde and dumb, and give good phone. She was a little disappointed to find a brunette at the desk, though clearly a shapely one, with the kind of breasts behind a blouse that Sharon herself had presented to the world before her two pregnancies. She censored that train of thought and walked up to the desk and said, "Excuse me. I need to see Hamish right away."

The brunette had been typing. She looked up and said, "You must be Mrs. Gibson." Then she went back to whatever form she was filling out on the screen.

Sharon said, "Yes. That's right. And it's urgent."

The secretary closed off the form, turned. She said, "Sorry about that, but you know how it is. You get halfway through and forget to save, and poof, it's all gone. He said you'd be coming in, but he didn't say when. I'm afraid he's with a client right now."

"Look," said Sharon, not being able to stop herself from noticing the hint of décolletage and the coy tilt of the head, and think how much men like Hamish go for that shit. "Really. I don't care if he's meeting with Elvis Presley. I need to see him now."

The brunette smiled then, that smile without words that said volumes to Sharon, "Get it through your head, you're the EX now, EX as in who gives a shit about you anymore. He's in my bed now, sweetie."

Sharon strode past her, opened the door to Hamish's office, and walked in. He did have a client in his office, a short bald man wearing a blue suit, an open brief case by his chair. Hamish was behind his desk, a pen in hand, poised above some documents. She saw that it was the Montblanc she had given him on his fortieth. She stopped, said, "I'm sorry to interrupt."

He looked at her. "I'm having a meeting here, Sharon."

She held her ground, glancing around the office, noticing the expensive furnishings and thinking about how much he whined over his child support payments.

She said, "This is important."

"God almighty, Sharon. Can't it wait ten minutes? You can see we're busy."

Taking a step farther into the office and standing over Hamish's client, looking him in the eye, and trying for her best woman-in-distress look, she said, "I'm sorry to interrupt. I truly am. I'm Sharon Gibson, Hamish's most recent ex-wife. And we have a family crisis to discuss. If you would just leave us alone for about twenty minutes, I would appreciate it."

The bald man raised his eyebrows at Hamish, but Hamish could only shrug. He got up quickly, fussed with his briefcase for a second, took it with him and left the office.

She looked at Hamish, seeing him now, his new spiked top haircut. She said, "You've got gel in your hair."

He ignored this and said, "Okay. Now, what the hell is this about it can't wait? I'm sure he has an explanation for the money. I'll get it out of him on the weekend."

"You remember what you gave Chris for his thirteenth birthday?" She didn't sit. He leaned back in his leather chair.

"Jesus H. Christ. Did you barge in here just to play Trivial Pursuit?"

"Do you remember?"

"No. I don't remember."

"You gave him a hunting knife."

"A hunting knife."

"One of those survivalist knives—doubles as a saw, fishhooks in the handle—the kind of thing every suburban kid needs. Along with four-by-fours, assault rifles. Do you remember now, Hamish?"

"And why is it important I remember?"

"We argued about it at the time. I said you were just perpetuating this male aggressive/macho bullshit. You said it was harmless. A Daniel Boone fantasy, that's all. I said I didn't want the thing in my house. You said, 'Our house, it's our house, sweetie.' Those were your exact words."

"Your memory amazes me, Sharon."

"It's the way it is, Hame. Women remember things. Men conveniently forget." She sat in the chair recently occupied by his client and took a breath.

"Okay. I won't argue. If I bought him a hunting knife, I bought him a hunting knife. But what's your point? Are we getting to some kind of point here?" He saw she was looking at the pen in his hand and put it down.

"The detectives showed me a picture of a knife they think killed Ms. Darnell. At least that was the point of their showing it to me, I think. And it looks to me just like that thing you gave Chris four years ago."

"You're losing me, Sharon. Darnell is the woman? I mean the woman's body you found at the school, right? What the hell has it got to do with my son?"

She ignored the "my" and said, "All right. I'll take it from the top for you, and I'll only use two-syllable words." She saw him smile a little at that. It was, she recalled, his saving grace. He could be a pompous ass, but he could laugh at himself—sometimes.

Hamish held up his hand for a second while he picked up the phone and told the brunette, who turned out to be Cheryl, to apologize profusely to Mr. Cairns and get him a coffee. This was going to take a little longer. He hung up, turned to Sharon, and said, "I'm all ears."

She said, "This could take a while. You sure your Mr. Cairns can wait that long?"

"That recent heavy rain did a little damage to his rumpus room. And he's trying to figure out how to squeeze a few thousand bucks for a home theatre system to go on top of the new carpet. He'll wait."

She took him through the events of the last couple of days. He didn't interrupt except for the occasional "Jesus Christ." And "I saw it on the news. I had no idea it had anything to do with..."

He asked her what she had told the detectives when they had shown her the picture of the knife.

She said, "Nothing. I didn't say anything. It took a while to sink in anyway. And I haven't seen that goddamn knife in his room for months, maybe a year."

That was when the phone rang and Cheryl told him there was a Detective Nash on the line, had told her to interrupt whatever he was doing. Hamish said, "All right. Put him on."

And then he heard the phone being handed over to someone, voices in the background, and then Christian's voice, saying, "Dad? The detective said I should call someone and I can't get Mom. Her cell is off."

# Fourteen

Alicia liked Dr. House. She adored Dr. House. Sharon hated the show. Still, to take her mind off Christian and the interminable, ponderous legal process that had taken over all their lives, she sat with Alicia to watch Dr. House solve another medical mystery. She told her daughter, as she had before, that if any doctor in a real hospital was as arrogant and disrespectful as House, the nurses would have him for breakfast. Besides, he's a walking invitation for a malpractice lawsuit. Alicia would say, "Can't you just enjoy the show ? Besides, Mom, it's not supposed to be reality. This is a TV drama. Fick-shun, not reality."

"And another thing," Sharon would say. "Look at them. A whole team of doctors with one patient. One patient. In a real hospital, we're running from one casualty to the next. Nobody gets that kind of attention."

Sharon would add—she didn't seem to be able to help herself—"And supposedly House is an internist, and he tells the surgeons when and who to operate on. That would be a day the earth stood still, when a surgeon allowed an internist to order him around. And besides, the great Dr. House doesn't really figure things out, make a diagnosis. He just tries out stuff to see if it works or kills the patient."

Sometimes, she seriously wondered why Alicia liked House the character. There was nothing likeable about him. She thought maybe it played to the adolescent mind. After all, House was constantly displaying the same attitude she got from Christian, and sometimes Alicia. Sarcasm, disdain, world-weary superiority, a more intellectual version of "whatever." Maybe the kids were watching House, thinking, *Hey, I can become a doctor without having to grow up first.* On the other hand, she smiled to herself; she'd known a few.

And to be fair, neither of her children was giving her that world-weary shit these days. Especially Christian. He was a different kid now, after a month in the young offenders unit at the detention centre.

She reached over, pulled her daughter to her, and hugged her. Alicia didn't resist or comment. She seemed to understand her mother's need. Sharon noted the time on the cable menu. Chris would be back in his cell now, lights out. He might have watched *House* too, with a dozen or so other young offenders in the common area. She hadn't seen the range, or his cell, but he'd described it to her on one of her visits. It sounded like any other jail, with the exception of none of the prisoners being over seventeen. A few meeting rooms, cells, a common area they called the range, an area the guards hung out, a shower room. Before his teens, Chris had actually been a little fastidious; she imagined how much he hated the lack of privacy now.

She had gone to the police station with Hamish, and they'd been reassured at first that Christian was just a "person of interest" in the case, not to worry. She had turned to Hamish and asked, "What the hell does that mean?"

He had said, "It means...I don't know what it means. I think it means they get to interview someone without actually charging him, reading his rights and shit. You know, they say they're just having a talk here, no need to have a lawyer present. We're all friends just trying to get to the bottom of the puzzle."

Chris was just old enough they didn't have to have his parents in the room when they talked with him, so Sharon and Hamish waited, went for coffee. Hamish seemed preoccupied, puzzled. He was off his game; he'd lost all that confidence he exuded in his own high-back leather chair. Sharon saw, surprised by this, that he was looking to her for guidance. Though maybe she shouldn't be surprised. Understanding men was always a matter of figuring out what was real and what was fake. How many of those ER docs would make a decision, state a fact, a diagnosis, then glance at her surreptitiously to see if she approved? She said, "Person of interest, suspect. Either way, he needs a lawyer. We have to get him a lawyer. Hamish."

He had brought two coffees over to their table in the nearby Tims. He said, "Yes. Sorry. I've never been in this situation before. I have no idea. He wasn't at the appointment you had with Ms. Darnell, were supposed to have with her, I mean. And he didn't know about the appointment?"

"No. He hadn't been home all night as far as I could see from the way his bedroom looked." She didn't tell him about the apparition she had seen at the end of the hall, in the fading light, the form, the shadow of a boy, a young man.

Hamish said, "He couldn't have done it. He just couldn't have.

He doesn't have it in him to do that sort of thing."

Sharon wasn't sure if that was a criticism or a simple observation. Christian had once been a good, skilled hockey player, but had backed away from it, given it up. Hamish had thought it happened when the game got tough, when contact was allowed, that his son just didn't have the heart for it. Sharon thought he'd given it up when Hamish left the home, a sort of "if Dad doesn't give a shit about anything, why should I?" response.

"God knows," said Sharon. "I know he didn't do it. In my heart, I know it. But who knows if we're not all capable of murder?"

Hamish looked at her then, in a way that said, "Maybe you, sweetie." When they were together, lived together, were married, she reminded herself, she'd sometimes tell him stories from the city, the less savoury side of the city, the side she ran into in the emergency, the father who tried to run his son over after an all-night drinking party, the things men put on their penises and the women put in their vaginas had to be pulled out or cut off, the knifings over a gram of cocaine, even a baggy of marijuana, the women beaten black and blue saying they tripped, their boyfriends coming to get them, needed their suppers cooked for them. He hadn't really wanted to hear those stories, and he sometimes pointed this out to her, and maybe she told them just because he didn't want to hear them. He had often said, "You have enough seniority now to take an administrative position, get away from all that shit."

She had said, "Hamish, he needs a lawyer. We need to find him a good lawyer."

Then they'd argued a little. She had said, "He needs a good criminal lawyer. Like the one in the paper all the time, defending drug dealers, rapists. Someone who really knows what he's doing in these kinds of things."

He had said, "Chris isn't even charged with anything. He could call in a favour from one of his clients, guy had a small private practice." He had said, "The lawyer you're talking about probably doesn't take a shit without a ten-thousand-dollar retainer."

And he hadn't been charged at that point, so she had agreed, and Hamish had called his friend on his cell. Sharon's mood had not improved listening to one side of the conversation. As far as she could tell, Hamish's good buddy was reluctant to do anything without Chris being charged, seemed to think the on-call duty lawyer would be enough at this stage. Hamish came off the phone and told her that his friend had advised them to go back to the station, ask to see their son, and then take him home if he hadn't been charged. To call him back if he had been.

Back at Central Station, Detective Nash had taken them into a small meeting room. Sharon couldn't tell what was coming. These cops had a way of being inscrutable, the stony look, blank eyes, giving nothing away. But his first words when they sat down were, "Mrs. Gibson. Have you had any second thoughts about that photograph I showed you?"

Sharon looked at Nash's partner, Dobrowski, standing half in, half out of the doorway, and then at Hamish, who simply raised his eyebrows and squirmed. She said, "Yes. I have. I had to check with Hamish, Chris's father, first. I wasn't sure. But it is similar to the one Chris' father gave him several years ago. A boy's knife. A hunting thing."

Nash said, "Chris tells us he traded it for a few ounces of marijuana maybe nine months ago. Could you verify that, Mrs. Gibson?"

Sharon said, "Could I verify that? No. Of course not. I don't think I've seen that knife in his room for a couple of years, but he sure as hell wouldn't have told me if he traded it for drugs. But it's probably true. I know he's been smoking a lot of marijuana, maybe even daily. I do my best but they can get it everywhere these days. And I know he's sold other stuff to buy it. I'm sure if he said he traded that knife for weed nine months ago, then that's what he did. I know teenagers lie. They all lie. But our Chris is not a good liar. And he's not violent." She was aware she was talking too much, explaining too much. She took a breath, looked at Hamish.

Hamish was finally finding his feet. He joined in. His voice seemed strained, though, rehearsed. He said, "Look, Officer. If you're not charging my son with anything, he's coming home with me now."

And that's when Nash said, "Thing is, Mr. Gibson, we charged him a half hour ago. That knife is the murder weapon, and we're sure it belongs to your son."

Hamish wanted to argue the case then and there. He said, "There are a million knives like that one. And if he says he doesn't have it anymore, he doesn't have it."

Sharon, having trouble breathing, feeling the room reeling, said, "Can we see him? Please?"

# Fifteen

As a nurse, she knew that life can change in a second, in the blink of an eye. She had seen it a hundred times. One too many heavy boxes on the front-end loader, reaching for a last leaf in the gutter, absentmindedly saying sure when your sixteen-year-old asks if he can take the snowmobile for a spin, an unexpected rut in the road, a lightning strike during a little league game. But this?

Her emotions wouldn't settle. She replayed the scene in the main hall of the school over and over. The shadowy figure at the end of the corridor was too tall for Chris, or too short. He wasn't capable of murder. But maybe no one is and everyone is. Could she have done something earlier? He was still hurting from his parents' separation. She felt guilt, confusion, remorse. And she was angry at him, her own son sitting in jail. The same kid who wanted to sit in his mother's lap when he was thirteen. Anyone with half a brain could see he couldn't possibly have done it. That he was just a scared kid.

They had gone to a bail hearing, expecting that with enough surety, sufficient promises and restrictions, they would be able to take him home, to Hamish's house if not to hers. But the charge was murder in the second degree and this murder was front-page news.

Alicia hadn't been to school in three weeks. This good student, this confident fourteen-year-old, this child who worried about being late and displeasing her teachers, wasn't sleeping at night and having panic attacks in the morning. She tried going a few days early on, but came home and told her mother she couldn't stand it. They all looked at her. She could hear them whispering behind her back. Could she transfer schools, please, she meant it, please. Sharon would have sent her off to the private school on the mountain, the one next to Mohawk, if she had the money. Maybe in September, she decided, but for now, Alicia was bright enough. She could afford to miss a couple of months.

There was another court date coming up next month, in May, this one to determine if the Crown had enough evidence to proceed to trial. Sharon was just now realizing how different the machinations of justice were in real life compared to *Law and Order*. Hearings to determine this and that, postponements, recesses, even court appearances to determine the date of the next court appearance, when both lawyers and judges might be back from Cancun. When she mentioned this to Hamish's friend when they retained him, he'd smiled and told them how difficult those TV dramas made it for everybody. Someone has a break-in, their laptop and a bottle of Scotch are stolen, the victims ask why the cops aren't dusting for fingerprints, sending in the crime scene crew to look for saliva they can test for DNA, run it through the computer back at the lab. Maybe even expecting babes in low cut lab coats, asking them a few questions.

They had retained Hamish's friend, Anthony (just-call-me-Tony) Clement, LLB, QC, who had reassured them he did have criminal trial experience. Sharon had said, "What about murder?" He had told them, "First degree assault, sexual assault, manslaughter. There aren't that many actual murder trials in this town."

Sharon didn't have the cash to retain a better-known criminal lawyer, like the one in the paper all the time, defending the obviously guilty. Hamish had been right, Tony confirmed. The star criminal lawyer would want a ten-thousand-dollar retainer, and he'd probably run through that very quickly. She couldn't do it on her own, and putting a big mortgage on the house she shared with Alicia was, well, a possibility if she had to. But Hamish's friend appeared to be okay, genuine, knew the legal processes, didn't charge them every time they phoned for some reassurance. He'd told them the evidence was pretty thin. They couldn't place Christian at the scene beyond what it ambiguously said in Ms. Darnell's computer, on her Outlook. And the knife in question was very common, thousands of them sold in Sporting Goods stores and Canadian Tire. But motive was a problem. Seems Darnell had a habit of calling in the parents and/or calling the cops she found a student doing, or worse, selling drugs. And there was no getting around it; the only possible source for that four thousand dollars was selling drugs.

Hamish was going to argue the point, but Tony just tilted his head a little, raised his eyebrows, and Hamish found he couldn't come up with anything plausible.

Sharon had asked if they knew anything about Ms. Darnell, like did she have a jealous lover, a gambling debt? Tony had said that was the detectives' job, look into all that. Their job was to defend Christian, and as far as he could see, they had lots of reasonable doubt going for them. He'd also suggested a psychiatric assessment might help get Chris out on bail, reassure the judge the kid wasn't a walking time bomb. It was their right to do this.

Sharon had sought out the psychiatrist who occasionally came down to the emergency department to see a kid who'd threatened to throw himself in front of a train, or a girl who'd told her school counsellor a voice was telling her to cut herself, and last month a sixteen-year-old who thought he was the son of God, or maybe it was the overdose of Ecstasy talking—a man with a surprisingly hearty laugh for a psychiatrist, most others she had known a bit reticent, stand-offish. With his white beard and paunch, he resembled, when he put on his reading glasses, none other than Santa Claus. Sharon wasn't sure this would reassure or terrify the kids he saw. Which reminded her how Alicia had jumped in the lap of the mall Santa Claus the first time, whereas Chris had hidden behind his mother's skirt and whimpered. This could not have been the four-year-old who grew up to commit murder.

As a juvenile offender, Chris' name had not been released to the press, nor the names of his parents, but Sharon assumed that everyone at the hospital would have put two and three together, that the gossip mill was working overtime, as it had at the high school Alicia no longer attended. So she was surprised when Dr. John Singleton had said, "That's your son? My oh my. It must be a terrible thing for a mother."

She was grateful he didn't say any more, didn't offer any false reassurance, but fell silent and waited for her. She knew from experience they were good at that, these shrinks, just sitting quietly, waiting. She had explained the situation, Chris being turned down for bail, and their lawyer suggesting a psychiatric assessment might help, if, of course, it offered an opinion that Chris was not a risk, not dangerous.

He had listened, nodding occasionally, but then he had explained, "No, really, I don't think you want a psychiatrist involved now, not yet. He's claiming he's innocent, right? Pleading not guilty. Now, the truth is that whether or not he's dangerous depends entirely on whether he did this thing or not. If not, then he's just another unpredictable teenager. But if he actually did it, then of course it means he is dangerous."

She had said, "It couldn't do any harm though, could it? I mean, if you saw him and found out that he didn't wet the bed or torture animals or hit his mother, that kind of thing?"

"I see you've been doing a bit of homework. But the problem is, Sharon, he's an adolescent. There was an episode on *Criminal Minds* recently, though maybe it was a rerun, anyway, one of the profilers saying to another something like, 'All teenagers profile as psychopaths.' That may be a bit of an exaggeration, but I'm sure if I saw him I would find that he's impulsive, that he's done his share of marijuana, if not other drugs, that he's not very good at planning sequentially, that he lacks empathy for others, and that he's somewhat egocentric, selfish. I might even find that he once tied a garter snake to a tree branch and shot arrows at it."

He paused when Sharon made a movement as if she were going to object to this characterization, but sighed instead. Dr. Singleton leaned back in his chair and said, "The snake thing was something I did as a kid, though the fact I remember it so clearly means I must have felt a little guilt at least, or a tiny bit of empathy for the snake. But look, he's a teenager. So I'm sure I'd find most of what I just described, and the Crown would have access to my report and he, or she, would neatly pick out those words and underline them for the judge: impulsive, egocentric, drug use, tortured snakes as a child, ignoring anything good I say about your son, of course. And then bail would be denied for sure. You only want a psychiatrist involved if Chris decides to plead guilty, or not criminally responsible due to mental illness. Then maybe I could help."

Sharon supposed what he had said was true. It made sense. But as she left, she couldn't quite shake the feeling that her Dr. Singleton, though maybe a good doctor, a clever psychiatrist, wanted nothing to do with this kind of court case. She knew many doctors hated going to court, being questioned about their opinions and diagnoses. One story had been the source of a good coffee room laugh a few months ago, the teller of the story doing a fair imitation of Dr. Singh's manner and accent. It seems Dr. Singh, an expert witness in a case, had offered his esteemed opinion. Opposing counsel had then asked the good doctor on what had he based this opinion. Was it on anything more than what the accused had told him? Dr. Singh had then drawn himself up and announced that he was a graduate of McGill University, had done postgraduate work at Stanford, was a member of the Royal College of Physicians and Surgeons in both Canada and Britain, and that he was board certified in New York and Michigan.

With a little smile, counsel had then asked, "And anything else, doctor?"

"Twenty-five years of experience," said Dr. Singh.

Chris remained in jail, in the juvenile wing, and Sharon visited twice a week. She hated these visits. There was no parking at the detention centre, but she found she could leave her car at the strip mall next door, near the dollar store, and join the half dozen or so girlfriends, mothers, sisters waiting in line outside the visitors' entrance. They waited on a covered walkway, sheltered from the rain, but still exposed on one side if the morning was cold and the wind harsh. She wondered about these young women, sometimes pushing baby carriages; the boys and men they were visiting demonstrably losers, unlikely to ever be good fathers and husbands. But there she was as well, visiting her son, who, she was sure, would one day grow into a fine man, though what that meant, she was no longer sure. She felt a wave of sympathy for the girls in front of her then, and the one coming up the walk now, a four-year-old in tow. If women weren't perennially optimistic, what would become of the world?

Her own mother had always been sure her husband would one day get through the Christmas season without drinking, picking a fight, and storming out of the house, leaving Sharon and older brother Gerald never sure there would be a Christmas morning, their father often not returning for three days, and mother taking to her bed. And her mother was always sure her oldest, Gerald, would grow out of this phase or that, the phases being, variously, refusing to go to school, coming home drunk or high, or stealing money from her purse.

Standing in line, Sharon wrestled with feelings that butted against one another. She and these other women were in the same boat, human beings, women, born to grief and hope, and waiting for their men. But she was always dressed a little better than these girls, and she wouldn't have a tattoo showing in the small of her back over a pair of track pants if she were to bend down to pick up a child or tie her laces. They were different, these girls and her. They came from a whole different world than she did. Or maybe not.

Then, a lawyer would walk briskly past them, not once looking in their direction, jumping the queue to announce himself at the intercom. Always simply his name, and "here to see my client." The first door would offer a soft buzz and click, and the lawyer would leave them behind in the line, waiting for 10:00 a.m. to arrive, the start of family visiting hour, unless there was a lockdown, which all too frequently occurred. For a moment, Sharon would see herself in the lawyer's eyes, just another poor, deluded woman standing in a short line for a brief visit with a husband, boyfriend, or son who might be guilty or innocent but sure as hell was not dependable. Another wave of sympathy passed over her, but then her turn came for the intercom, to push the button, announce that she was the mother of an inmate, here for a visit. She had trouble saying the word *inmate*, more comfortable with the word *patient*, but no substitute came to mind. She rejected *prisoner* and *resident* and always said *inmate* at the intercom as if there were quotation marks at either end, though even then saying the word always underscored the reality.

She had learned to leave her purse and bracelets at home, so she would only have her car keys to set the metal detector off. That was the routine: once through the narrow archway, hearing the bell, going over to the window and putting her keys in a small container, going back, and trying the archway again. If it didn't go off this second time, the attendant would buzz her through the second door.

She would then stand before the small speaking hole and the sliding metal tray separating the waiting area from the reception office, and wait for the correctional officer behind the heavy glass partition to look up from her computer. Once again she would announce whom she was here to visit, "Christian Gibson, my son," and place her driver's licence in the sliding metal tray.

Though a computer monitor sat on the desk in front of her, the officer would then look through a long list on a clipboard until she found, indeed, that one Christian Gibson was currently residing in the young offenders unit. Sharon's driver's licence would be returned to her in the metal tray, along with a visitor's tag to clip to her lapel. On her first visit, she found that she would have to leave her purse in a locker, and so on subsequent visits, she only brought her licence and other identification in a pocket-sized wallet. There was still another sheet to sign, with time in, and later time out, and the purpose of her visit, her relationship to the inmate, and then she would fasten the tag so it dangled in a readable fashion from her jacket, and take a seat in the waiting area.

An odd assortment of visitors waited with her on the hard plastic chairs, the chairs joined and secured to the floor. Some were clearly family members, exuding impatience, worry, embarrassment, usually a lawyer or two, exuding mostly impatience, almost always a Sally Ann or a New Age pastor with guitar and ingratiating smile, and some she couldn't figure, maybe a counsellor from the Six Nations Reserve, or a rehab officer, or John Howard staff.

The next part was just as she had watched many times on television, too many times she realized, and she also knew that from now on she would experience such scenes a little differently. She'd be called, and then escorted into a larger room with multiple chairs along a dividing glass wall with partial cubicles, where she could speak to Chris through an opening, an officer standing behind them all. She did not, she would not, ask him directly if he was innocent, truly innocent of this crime. She was terrified that he might deny it and she would know that he was lying. On the other hand, if she didn't ask, he might ask her why she didn't ask. But on her first visit, when she didn't ask, he said to her, "Mom, I swear to God, I didn't do it. I swear to God."

She had turned away when he said that, not wanting to look into his eyes lest she glimpse a truth she didn't want to see. Chris, like many of his friends, was fond of using that phrase. "I swear to God I didn't take your ten dollars. I swear to God I didn't have anything to drink at the party. I swear to God I didn't smoke any marijuana. Okay, I did share a bong at the party but I swear to God I didn't do any drugs." Chris seemed aware of this too, and how it weakened his current heartfelt denial, so he added, "Really, Mom. For real this time."

When she looked at him and said, "I know, Chris. I know.," he started to cry, snivel really, melting into a ten-year-old before her eyes. She wanted to touch him, hold him, this child of hers.

She glanced at the other inmates on his side of the glass, boys really, but some with shaved heads, multiple tattoos, talking to girlfriends, a disproportionately mixed-race group, Asian, Black, Indian, white. They all looked much tougher than her Chris, though maybe not bigger. And they all wore, like Chris, orange jump suits. She imagined the choice of colour and style had been based on the notion that these, both colour and style, would be the least likely ever freely chosen by a sane and sober human being, and so would always, without fail, signify the status of the wearer. She had tried to lighten the moment and had told him that orange was definitely not his colour. But he had simply responded,

"Mom, you gotta get me out of here. I can't stand it anymore. I really can't. I swear to God."

She never knew on subsequent visits whether she'd find her son, the ten-year-old now seventeen, on the other side of the glass, or this new alien kid who didn't have much to say, putting on a bit of a swagger for the benefit of his fellow prisoners, and telling her it was cool, it was all cool, she didn't have to worry about him, really Mom. And, "Tell Dad he doesn't have to visit. He hates coming here, I can tell."

Alicia always asked her mother how her brother was holding up, after these visits, but she never asked to go along. Sharon was grateful for this, not sure her answer should be yes or no. She also wondered, after her visit with Dr. Singleton, if Alicia had imagined her schoolmates talking about her, about Chris, or if they really knew.

Sharon hadn't taken a full leave of absence from the hospital, but had been allowed to cut back to three nights a week, in the circumstances, without losing benefits or pension. Hamish at least—she assumed, because neither she nor he had brought up the subject—would cover the cost of Just-call-me-Tony Clement.

She almost called her brother, the one drinking his life away in the bars of Sudbury, waiting for the nickel mines to hire again, or maybe it was uranium, but the last time she had seen him she had told him they would have no further contact, none, nada, I mean it, those were her words, "Until you're clean and sober for six months." "Ah, sis," he'd said, at the time in his maudlin phase, the one that preceded paranoid rage during his binges. She almost called him because she was sure he'd seen the inside of a jail or two, though she didn't know for sure, and might, what? Might have some advice for Chris? No. She didn't need him around, Gerald, big brother, in trouble from the moment he turned thirteen, but a sweet man when he wasn't doing drugs or drinking.

When drinking, he could riff for hours on the unfairness of the "system," as he called it, seeming to include everything from his birthright, through the current political party in office, to capitalism and free trade. No, she said to herself, he wouldn't be any help. And Chris sure as hell didn't need his uncle Gerald in his life as a—she shuddered at the cliché—a male role model.

But thinking of her brother raised in her mind the possibility her Chris had inherited the same propensities, that this had come from her side of the family. Maybe her brother's need to quell anxiety, what had he called it? To quell the heebie-jeebies with alcohol, but not the rage. No. She'd never seen Chris rage, be destructive, as she had witnessed her brother in his teens. Their father had made an effort, buying the wall board and spackle, supervising Gerald while he repaired the holes in his bedroom wall that he had made with his fist the night before, their father usually becoming impatient with his son's poor skills, and eventually saying, "Here. Give it to me. You're making a mess of it."

She knew her mother still talked to Gerald, still believed he'd some day find a nice girl and settle down, though now fifty-two and beginning to show the ravages of years of smoking and drinking. As Mother saw it, he had chosen to be a bachelor, and his unemployment had always been a product of the economic times and nothing to do with his drinking, though she did admit he had a small problem with the bottle, being alone and all.

Their mother had remarried a man she'd met in Florida during an excursion of widows and widowers. "He has property there," she announced. "He's very well off, and a real gentleman." Sharon immediately suspected she'd met a man who actually had his eye on her mom's property, her house in Winona, because at first they had moved in there together, and stayed through a summer, and his background remained mysterious to Sharon, as it was to her mother. But as it turned out, he did have a small house in Englewood, near Venice, and this man, Fred, officially now, she supposed, her stepfather, and her mother, had settled into a common enough retirement plan: 180 days in subtropical Florida, avoiding the harsh Ontario winter altogether, without losing medical benefits, and summers in Winona. Which was where they would be now.

When she had first heard about the relationship with Fred, who may have been retired from the armed forces or maybe the CIA, some job he didn't or couldn't talk about he would say mysteriously, she had said, "Okay, Mom, if he makes you happy. But for God's sake, don't lend him money or marry him."

"Of course not, dear. I wasn't born yesterday, you know."

But of course she had done both. So the Winona house was now communal property, and she suspected her mother's savings were near depletion, but she was happier with Fred than she had been alone, perhaps happier than she had been with Sharon's father those last years. Sharon backed off. Her mother's savings were not that substantial anyway. A house was just a house; she had herself to sort out after divorcing Hamish, and a younger generation to worry about.

Sharon and her mother talked on the phone once a week, and so far, as far as her mother was concerned, life proceeded uneventfully for her daughter the nurse, the single parent of two, and as always she would plan her vacation time this year so that she could visit, with both her teenagers in tow, pulling them away from their friends, for a week or two in August, or maybe during the Peach Festival. "Chris, oh, he's fine. He's off with a friend at the moment. I think they're skateboarding. Would you like to speak with Alicia? I'll see if I can tear her away from Dr. House."

# Sixteen

They'd been at this four weeks now, and it had become tedious, Jerome coming out of the small kitchen saying, "Fuck, that's nigger work. Don't you know any little *chicas* could do this? Find a bigger kitchen, maybe?"

Sal had said, "You say nigger a lot, like you a brother, but I suspect they scare you, *compadre*."

Jerome was actually curious now. He said, "I always wondered, being from El Salvador, if you got Indian in you, or just Spanish and African?" His vow to remain a seller and not a user had lasted maybe a week, though it was under control, not like he needed it or nothing, just reasonable he should sample the product daily, make sure the batch was up to company standards. His probation appointments were regular now, with urine tests on a schedule, so as long as he remembered the dates, and abstained for two days, he'd be all right, problem being one of thinking ahead at least three days.

"Who knows?" said Sal. "Maybe what's left is an eighth Spanish, where I get my nose."

Jerome showed up each day about noon. He thought of coming earlier, but that would feel like he was employed by Sal, not being his partner in this. He did the cooking while Sal went out to score some cocaine. He didn't ask Sal where he went, assumed he had a source he wouldn't reveal anyway. Jerome turned the cocaine into crack on the gas stove, watching over it, actually finding some pleasure doing the job well, with as little wasted as possible.

Cocaine to crack increased the value by a factor of ten, a markup of ten times. Jerome remembered someone telling him, "Shit, the only commodity that beats that markup is bottled water. They're the real criminals here, buying city tap water, running some radiation over it, maybe just passing it through a magnet or something, putting it into little plastic bottles and marking it up, what? Two thousand percent, at least. Now that is usury, man, usury." He had read the label on one of those bottles after being told that, noticed it said, "Spring Water," whatever the hell that meant, and that the company bottling this stuff was a very good citizen, environmentally conscious, and had reduced the size of the plastic cap by one third. Whoopdee fucking dee. That should save the planet.

He'd seen on the Discovery Channel there were places in the ocean, the currents circling for some reason, accumulating billions of these bottles, just floating along. And they'd call him a criminal, just cooking up a little crack to sell to anxious customers, help his customers forget their problems, get laid easier. Selling it direct, not putting it into little plastic bottles or baggies would last forever. Okay, the crack isn't exactly harmless, but everybody's got a choice, like himself: do it, don't do it. Drink bottled water or city water. It's a free country, man. A fucking free country, he'd said to himself, taking a small sampling, snorting some of the white powder didn't make it into the pot.

Sal, getting the pipes ready for the influx of afternoon customers, was still pondering Jerome's question of heritage. He said, "I'm sure I have some African in me, not the tall ones, though. What are they, Watusi, Somalian, and maybe you do too, your black hair. I know you wonder why I don't react you use the word 'nigger.' It is because nigger is not a race. It is a concept. In El Salvador, and Costa Rica, the niggers are Nicaraguans, mostly Indian, have to do the nigger work.

"I asked my momma one time," said Jerome, "did my hair come from Cree Indian? The only likely intruders might have roosted sometime in the family tree. My momma said that's a possibility, but I think of you as my Highlander, got some of your grandmother's Scottish blood in you. The clan MacGregor or some shit. But you, you got African in you, I think, though it's gotta be pygmy from the Congo." As he said this, his tongue loosened by the sniff of cocaine he'd taken before coming out of the kitchen, Jerome wondered if he'd pushed it too far, would finally get a nasty reaction from cool Sal.

But Sal smiled at this, said, "No, those conquistadors maybe looked tall coming off the beach in spiky helmets, but they was short *hommes*, just little Spanish *pisanos*, coming to take our gold and give us syphilis."

One full month now. Jerome was aware this was the longest time he'd spent with anybody, any one person, every day, not counting jail time, or his momma. Some days when they weren't probing each other, they'd talk about politics or what's on the news. Not that they had any in-depth discussions of an intimate nature, but it was fucking uncomfortable just the same, like they were married or some shit. He'd had a few steady relationships with women, but never every day. Maybe he'd been able to tolerate three days in a row, tops, but after that he'd have to get the fuck out for while, get away from the talking. Man, can women ever talk. Didn't matter they were junkies or clean, they still talked about every-fucking-thing, and not just one time, but before they'd do it, when they were doing it, and after they were through doing it. He'd go find himself a hooker. She'd ask what he'd like, she gave a pretty good blow job. Jerome would say, "That'd be fine, you keep it in your mouth you can't talk at the same time."

Jerome said, "They got some seventeen-year-old kid for the teacher, but they don't tell his name, you see that?"

Sal looked up. Jerome had turned on the television, was watching a local news channel. He said, "I see that."

"You think she gave him a bad mark, kept him off the football team?"

"I think had nothing to do with that."

"They arguing about it. The prosecutor, what d'ya call it, the Crown, wants to try the kid as an adult, give out his name."

Sal said, "I know his name."

Jerome turned from the TV then, said, "Yeah?"

"I think was a kid who sold for me awhile. Before I do it this way."

Jerome said, "I was thinking about that. Why not have the kids do the selling? Pick a few of the tough ones, give 'em a try. Like that story I seen on TV one time, a musical. Not the Scrooge thing. The other one."

Sal said, "You cannot trust them. They got some of your product in their pockets they think maybe they try some, or take some off the top. That age, they not so good at figuring what will happen next, you know it. Figure they can talk their way out of anything."

Jerome said, "So what's the kid's name? The one they got for the teacher?"

The intercom buzzed then, announcing their first customer of the day. Sal said, "You take this one."

Buzzing some kid in, watching through the fisheye, Jerome said, "How long you think we get away with this, before someone wonders why all those boys and girls hanging out in front?"

Sal said, while getting a pipe ready, "They pack animals, these teenagers. The ones you gotta worry about are the ones hanging out alone."

# Seventeen

*He doesn't look like much*, was Sharon's first thought when she saw him enter the coffee shop. She had asked on the phone, "How will I know you?" He had said, "I'll know you." *Fair enough*, she had thought, *I'll probably be the only forty-ish woman there alone, at least without a laptop using the Wi-Fi.* But he was the one who was obvious, entering alone, looking around for someone. It occurred to Sharon how easy it was to distinguish a man looking for a wife or lover or friend from someone looking for a stranger, not just scanning, but his eyes lingering long enough to make a difference.

He approached her table, said, "Sharon Gibson?" and sat down, extending a hand, and adding, "Ben Walters," all in one movement. She had a café mocha in front of her on the small round table. He looked at it and then said, getting up again, "Why don't I fetch myself a coffee first? Then we can talk."

On the phone she had asked why they wouldn't first meet in his office, assuming he had one, and he had explained he always held the first meet—he used the shortened word—in a coffee shop. "It's less intimidating, and besides, in my line of work, it's not always wise to let prospective clients know where I live."

She imagined this meant he worked out of his home, but then, why wouldn't you these days? She had been mildly disappointed about this, having conjured in her mind the kind of office occupied by the private detectives of her imagination, the Mike Hammers and Mickey Spillanes, or even Dennis LeHane's Kenzie—creaky wooden floors, transom doors, old filing cabinets, a rotary dial telephone on a wooden desk and a window looking down into the streets of 1940s Los Angeles.

She had said to Alicia, "I need to hire a private detective. But how on earth do you go about doing that?"

Alicia had said, "Is there such a thing in real life?"

Sharon had paused for a moment, thinking how these days there might be a shortage of long-legged heiresses with missing husbands, and birds filled with jewels. She said, "Of course there are, but I think they mostly spy on philandering husbands, or take pictures of disabled people dancing the polka."

Alicia had said, "You could ask Dad."

She had chosen Google instead, first Ontario, then narrowed to Hamilton, where she found a surprising number of listings, though no Pinkertons. Some were specialized in precisely the activities she had, somewhat tongue in cheek, described to Alicia, while others did mention "missing persons," "fraud," and "criminal matters." Two claimed to be retired police officers, but both focused on "child custody issues," and Sharon wondered how they might receive her explanation for the need of their services, being that the real cops were not doing their job.

The impetus for all of this had arisen from her visit with Detective Harry Nash. She had asked point blank, "Are you pursuing any other possibilities, any other leads?"

He had said, "I can't discuss any details with you, Mrs. Gibson, but of course we're looking at other possibilities." Then he had sat there watching her, waiting.

She had blurted out, "Chris did not do this thing, this horrible thing. So someone else did. Are you at least considering other possibilities? A student with a grudge, something in her personal life?"

He said, "We've looked into all of it, Mrs. Gibson. I can assure you this case isn't closed."

She was sure he had lied to her, and it made sense, of course. If the Crown had gone out on a limb charging Chris, then he wouldn't want detectives nosing around undermining his case. No. She came away from the meeting pretty sure they thought they had their man, or boy in this case, and were just looking for more evidence to support this.

Right after Chris's arrest, they had arrived back at the house with a warrant, looked more carefully through his room, and had taken away some items of clothing and the almost four thousand dollars from his sweater drawer. When she had asked him, again, point blank, if they had any further evidence, did they have Chris's DNA on the knife or anything like that, Nash had said he couldn't discuss that kind of detail with her, but the prosecution was obliged to disclose all the evidence they had to the defence attorney in a timely fashion.

In the weeks following the murder and Chris's arrest, it had gradually dawned on Sharon that something was missing from the newspaper reports. The teachers had organized a memorial service for Ms. (it had turned out to be Philomena) Darnell. Several students had been interviewed about their trauma, their fears and reactions, and Ms. Darnell came across as a dedicated teacher, beloved by her students, respected by her colleagues.

Articles appeared on school safety, about the possible need for more security, even metal detectors, and these articles, in internet form, had generated heated discussion, but at no time had there been any mention of family. The victim's family. And Sharon knew reporters liked to find grieving family members and ask that most stupid of questions, "How do you feel...?"

Ms. Darnell was, had been, a single woman, with no husband or children, but surely someone had been notified. A sister, a parent, a distant cousin? And Sharon was pretty sure that today, had the reporters found a same-sex partner or lover, they would have reported that as simple fact and at least tried to interview the woman.

Sharon had mentioned all this on the phone with Ben Walters, and now, having returned with a regular coffee, black, two packets of raw sugar, emptied one into his coffee and stirred, he said, "I checked and you're right. The victim is something of a mystery."

*He's about fifty-five*, she thought, with a small grey moustache, salt and pepper hair in what was once called a brush cut, wearing an open shirt under a simple jacket. She found the gold chain around his neck a little disconcerting. He opened his small briefcase to take out a blank pad of paper, and then retrieved both a pen and his reading glasses from his shirt pocket. He said, "Now you're sure you want me looking into this? I could find more evidence against young Chris."

Sharon said, "I know Chris didn't do it. He's a..." She caught herself about to say, "He's a good boy." And then changed this to "He doesn't have it in him to do violence."

"Look," said Walters. "Every time I have to hang around the courthouse, I see mothers in the second row saying something like that about their sons standing there before the judge. He's really a good boy, my Jocko."

"I know my son."

"You think Mrs. Bundy didn't say that about her Teddy?"

Sharon said, "Maybe I'm wasting your time."

"I'm sorry. I just want to make sure you understand the possibilities, that's all."

"You mean the possibility that my son actually did this?"

"Yes."

"It's with me every minute of the day, Mr. Walters."

He took a long drink of his coffee then, made a face at its bitterness and added the second packet of sugar. He said, "Okay. You are probably right. Once they've arrested someone, they're not going to look too hard for a different suspect. They find someone else with a possible motive, for instance, the defence can use that in court."

"But where on earth do we start?" asked Sharon.

"With the victim," he said. "With the victim."

It was a warm day in May and the few servers had opened the umbrellas above the tables on the patio. Sharon noticed the new customers were taking their café lattes and biscotti outside to enjoy in the clear air. She and Ben sat inside, Sharon becoming increasingly pessimistic. He explained he charged two hundred dollars a day plus expenses, and when she raised her eyebrows, he added, "But for single working mothers, I discount my fee to $150 a day." She noticed he enjoyed looking at her and suspected that was the source of his generosity, but $50 was $50. He went on to explain expenses meant out-of-pocket expenses, such as having to pay an informant for information. And he would need $1000 up front, and she would receive an itemized account from him weekly.

She started to ask him if he thought this would work, or help, or prove her Chris innocent, but she didn't know how to word the question. She knew she was only looking for reassurance and Mr. Walters did not appear to be in the reassuring business. The business she had been in most of her professional life. Everything will turn out fine. This will only hurt for a second. I'm sure it's nothing, just a virus. The doctor has ordered some blood tests to be certain.

But she was impressed when he told her that before they met, he had *ascertained*–that was the word he used. A little pompous, she thought—he had ascertained the victim's place of residence and that's where he would go first, see what he could find.

She said, "I'll come with you."

He had said, "No. That wouldn't be smart. Can you imagine what the police would make of the accused's mother rifling through the victim's home?"

She had said, "My son has been charged with a murder, Mr. Walters. I don't give a goddamn what anybody thinks. I'm going with you."

# Eighteen

They had taken two cars to the address Walters had shown her, a four-storey brick apartment block on King East, the kind of residence Sharon associated with welfare recipients. She had thought at first that the inside might be more impressive. The building, though run down on the outside and located on a busy unidirectional throughway, was of a generation of spacious rooms and high ceilings, built when the throughway had been a two-way street, maybe with a streetcar or tram.

Walters simply pushed intercom buttons until someone buzzed them in before asking questions. The foyer and hallways turned out to be no more, perhaps less, impressive than the exterior. Ms. P. Darnell's apartment was on the second floor, facing the street.

When they had climbed a flight of stairs and arrived at her numbered wooden door, Walters had said, pulling an instrument from his jacket pocket, "This is your chance to go home, or wait outside, before we, and I emphasize 'we,' commit a criminal act."

She had said, "And I thought you were just gonna ask the super for a key."

She saw that it took him a half second to recognize the sarcasm, but he had shrugged and picked the lock in a manner that appeared to Sharon quite practised. Once inside, he said, "The police have undoubtedly been here, but they weren't looking for what we're looking for."

"And what are we looking for?" asked Sharon.

"We'll know when we find it," he said.

It was a spacious two-bedroom apartment with hardwood floors and original gumwood trim, dating the building perhaps to 1930, or just after the First World War and before the Great Depression.

Sharon stood in the living room, separated by an arch from a dining area. It was all a bit...she searched for a word...*dowdy* came to mind. *Lived-in* for sure, a teacup still sitting by an armchair. Nothing on the walls to indicate a family.

She followed Walters into what looked like a bedroom converted into a home office: computer, printer, desk, piles of papers, a filing cabinet.

Walters said, "She had a thing about drugs, I see. Recognize any of these names?"

He handed her the papers and snapshots he had been looking at, lists of names with notations beside them. "Using," "Possible stoned first period," "Suspected selling." Some of the photos showed single teens lounging, a group around some kind of fire pit, two in conversation. They were unclear, taken from a distance, but usually included at least one of the kids vaping, or lighting a cigarette or joint.

"She was on a crusade, I think. Fits with what my daughter told me."

"More like an obsession," said Walters.

It was in the poor woman's bedroom that Sharon found the photo, the printout of Chris. Chris and some man. The man a foot shorter, but some kind of exchange taking place, arms outstretched. For a moment, she forgot to breathe. Then she let out a long unintelligible oath, some combination of shit and fuck, and sat heavily on the bed.

Walters watched her, then sat beside her. He nudged her with his shoulder. Her head drooped. Then he lifted her face to his and moved in to kiss her.

"Jesus. No. For Christ's sakes. What the hell are you thinking?" She was on her feet now, crumbling the photo and throwing it at Walters. "What the hell are you thinking? Not now. Not here. Fuck, fuck, fuck."

Once back in her car, she took a breath, waited, and thought of the noise she had made, yelling, then storming off, slamming the door. And wondered if anyone had heard her, or seen her, and did it matter? She had seen it. Evidence of Chris doing what? What the hell has he been doing?

Two bottles of white wine. That was it, all she could find in the liquor cabinet, her liquor cabinet being simply one of the cupboards under the kitchen counter. It would have to do. That and some shit on TV. Something without drugs and crime.

When she had arrived home, her mind still running through her very own B and E, she found Alicia halfway out the front door, asked, "Where are you off to?"

And Alicia had simply answered, "Nice of you to come home, Mother."

"Alicia. Where are you going?"

"I'm gonna hang out with Maureen. Maybe stay over."

"Can we have supper first? Together?"

"I already ate, Mother."

Calling Sharon "Mother" twice in half a minute. "All right. All right. Phone me when you get there, okay? And how are you getting there?"

"It's a short walk. I'll cut through the park."

And she was off, with Sharon calling after her, "Stay on the sidewalk, please."

# Nineteen

It had been a long afternoon and evening and Jerome was having second thoughts about this Dell computer approach to the distribution of illegal substances. Direct to the end user. Must work pretty well for Michael Dell, but not so good for the poor slubs have to do the actual delivery. He said, "So you had sellers before, but it didn't work out?"

"Why we met," said Sal.

"Yeah?"

"And..."

"And what?"

"It is not a story I am ready to tell," said Sal, looking, surprisingly, evasive.

Jerome was thinking, *So, not so cool after all.* He said, "You had that kid selling for you? What went down?"

"All right. I tell you. I have ahh, *de buen corizon*."

"What?"

"You don't see it, but I am not conquistador. I am not, as you say, ruthless."

"Yeah?"

"You got people working for you, know who you are, where

you live, you have to be *despiadado*. The people I buy from, they let you know, man. They let you know that."

Jerome said, "Yeah?"

"Those boys. Those young men think they have cojones. But they are stupid."

"And the teacher was killed?"

"She take pictures of the kids using."

"Yeah?"

"And then she show them and say she gonna show them to their mommas."

"That get her killed?"

"Maybe she had other pictures. Maybe the kids tell her too much."

"Did you do her, man?"

Sharon was into the second bottle when she reached for her cell and tapped on Hamish's number. He picked up quickly but said nothing.

Sharon said, "Hamish?"

"Hello, Sharon."

"Hamish, we have to do something...Hamish!"

"Are you all right?"

Sharon said, "No. I am not all right. How could I be all right?"

There was a pause before Hamish asked, "Have you been drinking...Sharon?"

"Is there someone there with you, Hamy?"

"You've been drinking, Sharon."

"So what if I have?"

"There's no point in trying to talk if you've been drinking."

"There's no point if I'm stone-cold sober, either."

"That's not...fair."

"So, can you get my son out of jail?"

"He's my son as well, Sharon."

"Well then, do something. Do fucking something."

"Like what?"

"Like, I don't know. Hire a better lawyer."

"There's nothing...there's fucking nothing..."

Sharon shifted on the couch, sat up straighter, took another sip of wine, and a breath, and then said, "Have you considered...?"

"Have I considered what?"

"That your son...that our son is...guilty?"

"I'm going to hang up, Sharon."

"No, you're not. No, you're not. Not while Chris is...not while Chris is..."

At that, she dropped the phone on a pillow, heard Hamish's muffled voice, his appeals, and then nothing.

"What the hell are you doing here?"

She must have dozed, her cell still face down on a pillow, a third of a bottle left, when some banging on the front door startled her. Had she been sober, stone-cold sober, she might have ignored the intrusion, threatened to call the police. But, not thinking clearly, she had stumbled to the door and opened it wide. And there was Ben Walters, looking a little off himself.

He said, "Wait. It's okay. It's okay. I came to apologize. I won't touch you. I won't come near you."

He was already a step inside as Sharon backed from the door, leaned against a wall. She said, "You're drunk."

"Your observation is accurate."

"And you stink."

"I had a shower."

"Metaphorically, you stink." She could hear herself stumble on the word. She slid down the wall and sat on the floor.

He sat on the floor beside her, not too close. "I came to apologize. I...fucked up."

"Yes, you did."

"I am sorry. It was not professional."

Sharon said, looking at him, "You tell me what it is about men. What is it about men that makes them screw up everything? Ruin every-fucking-thing."

"I didn't come at a good time, did I?"

"Not particularly." She heard herself slurring that word as well.

"I also came to say I'd keep looking into things for you."

"What's the point? Christian was selling goddamn drugs. That teacher, Darnell, she was going to tell me about it. Everything I find just helps their case."

"Wait a minute. Your kid was smoking pot. He was selling a bit of it. Doesn't mean he killed anybody.

"You were right the first time."

"Maybe I wasn't."

Sharon looked over at him, and around, aware they were two adults sitting on the floor of the small front hall, one of them drunk, maybe both of them. She said, "Take your coat off. I'll make us some coffee." She swung onto her knees and used the wall to help her get on her feet, determined to do it unaided.

# Twenty

The line up at the detention centre was not too long this morning, though Sharon did notice one girl who looked no older than Alicia, though had to be, she was sure, at least eighteen. In the waiting area, as usual, there were two smiling young men, come to lead the sinners to Jesus. The art teacher wasn't there today, the one she had met before who brought art books and held seminars for any inmates who chose to join. She wondered why on earth these young men would volunteer to attend a class on art appreciation, but then realized they would probably choose any kind of gathering to get off the range for an hour, and maybe expect to see a nude or two.

And she wondered who on earth running these detention centres believed that some Jesus exposure and art appreciation could change human behaviour.

She was a bit hung over and becoming cynical. She tried to think kinder thoughts. They were trying to help, after all.

She was able to see Chris across a table, a guard standing watch in the corner. Chris looked defeated. But he said, "I'm okay. I'm okay, Mom."

"You look like shit," she said.

"Nice talk."

"Chris, look, I have to ask you. To help you. Who was selling you drugs?"

"What? Nobody."

"Look. Chris. I know you were selling, so you had to be buying from someone. Someone up the ladder, I mean a real dealer. Give me a name."

"Holy shit. You sound like a narc."

"I'm trying to fucking help, Christian. The cops aren't looking for anybody else. I've seen a photo of you buying from somebody. Who was it?"

"What? A picture? No way."

"Yes, way. The teacher took it somewhere."

"Oh shit. Mom. I swear to God..."

"Do not swear to God at me. Just tell me the truth. This time. Please."

"But..."

"No buts. You bought enough to net at least four thousand dollars. I don't care what it was. Just who sold you the stuff in the first place."

"I wasn't doing much."

"Let me spell it out. I need the name of someone else who would have a motive to kill the teacher. The cops aren't looking. They probably haven't even asked you."

Chris looked away, then down at the table; his feet drummed the floor. "All right. But what are you gonna to do?"

"Leave that to me."

"Okay. All right." He leaned in a little. "A guy. Hispanic. I don't know his name."

"And?"

"And what?"

"At least where? Where were you buying?"

"There's like this apartment building, Upper Wentworth. Guy usually sells single pulls through a peephole."

"He does what?"

"It's like, you know, a crack pipe. Stuck through the eye thing in a door."

"And what?"

"You know, like the customers, they pass in some money and they get a long pull on the thing."

"Good God almighty."

"Yeah. I know it's stupid."

"Really stupid."

"Yeah, well…"

"And where do you come in?"

Outside the detention centre, Sharon took a deep breath. For a moment, she wondered if they purposely reduce the oxygen and increase the noise in jails. Random sounds bouncing off cement walls all day would drive anyone nuts. You'd think it would be a more successful deterrent. She stood for a minute, looking back at the building. Jails, prisons. Maybe better than beheadings and forty lashes. But she knew for some it became a badge of honour. Get the prison tats to mark the occasion. At least, so far, Chris looked sad, frightened, embarrassed.

In her car parked across the side street in the mall, next to the dollar store, she tapped on Alicia's number in her cell. Alicia answered quickly.

"Are you home?"

Alicia said, "Good morning, Mother."

"Did you have a good time with your friend?"

"Yeah, I got in an hour ago. There's no milk in the fridge, you know."

"I'll pick some up. I was visiting your brother."

"And there's no fruit left."

"Aren't you going to ask how he's doing?"

"I'm so angry with him. What did he...I mean, why did he... Like...How is he?"

"Not happy."

"Well, he...you know what they're saying?"

"Alicia. I'll be home later. Maybe an hour or two. Then we'll talk."

"What are you doing?"

"Just an errand. I have to run an errand. We'll talk when I get home. You be safe and stay home until I get there. You hear me?"

"Whatever."

"Alicia?"

"Okay. I'll be here."

Sharon found the address Christian had given her. At least the one building that matched his description in the block past the used car dealer he had also described. She parked on the street about 50 yards away and sat wondering what the hell she was doing here. What could she possibly accomplish? But...

It was an apartment building, six storeys, low income maybe, but respectable. A couple of teenage boys stood outside on the sidewalk by the path, trying to look, what, cool? Disinterested?

Tough? She watched as one of them walked to the main entrance, pushed a buzzer. The door unlocked and the boy entered, not glancing back. The second boy followed, but stayed outside at the entrance. Sharon left her car and walked in the direction of the entrance as nonchalantly as she could, which, she guessed, was really slow and self-conscious. But her timing was good. The first boy emerged, looking even more dazed than most teenage boys. The second pushed the buzzer once. The door unlocked. He went in, and Sharon quickly followed, stopping the door from locking with her foot, waiting a moment, and then entering. She was wearing her work shoes, the soft-soled casual tennis shoes that made twelve hours walking hospital corridors possible, and quiet.

The second boy walked down the long east corridor on the main floor. Sharon waited and watched. She saw him approach a door, knock once, stick what looked like a rolled bill into an eye hole in the door. A few seconds later, a stem of some kind appeared, and the boy leaned in and sucked on it. Just as Christian had described.

Jerome said, "This is fucking tedious, you know that."

Sal said, "It's a slow day." He was sitting in the only decent armchair, drinking a café con leche, reading the newspaper, like any semi-employed citizen might be doing on a slow Saturday morning.

Jerome said, "We gotta move up the chain in this business. Get us a sales force. Get us some real product."

Sal took a sip of his coffee, said, "All in good time. You doing much better than minimum wage, my friend. We move when the time is right. When it's safe."

"Yeah, but shit. I'm fucking bored to death."

Sal put his paper aside, said, "We move too fast, they send some moogs from Toronto to whack us. Or maybe kill your mamma."

"Why would they kill my mother? What the fuck would that get them?"

"They just not so smart. You know that. Here. In the news feed today. They whacked the parents of some guy they didn't like, in Brantford. Momma and Poppa. They was looking for this guy did 'em wrong, or disrespected them, or stole a bit off the top, something, they go to his parents' house. He's not there, so they kill both his parents. Must be hard to live with."

Jerome looked at him. "What's hard to live with?"

Sal said, "You raise a boy turns into an asshole is one thing. He gets you killed is another. And I think you got another customer."

Jerome stooped and looked through the eyehole. "Holy shit."

Sal said, "Holy shit what? If it might be a cop, just back away."

"I think it's that bitch nurse from the General. The one offered me fucking Advil for a kidney stone."

"You tell me that story. The lady got *cajónes*."

Jerome said, "What the fuck is she doing here?"

Sharon hesitated at the door and then, not knowing what else to do, simply knocked on it.

A voice from the other side of the door said, "Well, if it isn't Nurse Rat Shit, come to visit."

Sharon hesitated. Who the hell would know she's a nurse? But her mind focused on the cinematic trivia, the only nurse who ever made a pedophile sympathetic. "It's Nurse Ratched, not Rat Shit. And I think it was a pun on Wretched, not Rat Shit."

A second voice from the other side of the door said, "I like this bitch."

Sharon hesitated, then said, "How do you know I'm a nurse?"

"You the cunt gave me Advil for a life-threatening condition."

"Oh. Ah, sorry about that."

"Why the fuck are you here?"

"I just need some information."

"You see a sign above the door or something?"

"About my son. He said he was selling for you a while back."

Nothing was coming from the other side.

"They think he killed a teacher. I just want..." Sharon took a deep breath. There was no way of finishing that sentence. She wanted what? Find somebody else who did it? Like one of the men on the other side of the door? She told herself it was time to leave, but the door opened a foot, and the face was there. Her patient from the ER. But not her patient now, and she was suddenly very aware of this not being the hospital, her domain. This was their territory. But she remembered his name and said it.

"Mr. Waverly?"

He stared at her. She saw someone move behind him. The other voice said, "You stupid bastard. What'd I say? You never open the door."

Then the door opened wide, and they grabbed her arms and pulled her in, stumbling, and the door slammed shut.

Sharon backed against a wall, looked around. Waverly was there, and another man, shorter, darker skin. Her mind saw them as Mutt and Jeff. Then her natural reaction to medical emergencies took over, a calmness descended. She knew it should have been a flight or fight response, preferably flight, but this thing always happened. Calmness instead of fear. It served her well in medical emergencies, but maybe not in this world.

The shorter man, Hispanic probably, maybe the man Christian had described. He was looking her over.

The man called Waverly said, "What was your problem, bitch? A little oxy, a little morph to fix me up? No skin off your nose. The doc would order it. You just had to fucking deliver it."

Sharon said, "May I sit down?"

The other man said, "Of course, Senora. We are not barbarians."

Sharon sat in the armchair. Old hardwood floors, curtains closed on the one window in this main room. Doorway to a small kitchen. Another door, probably to a bedroom. The apartment of two men who had never in their lives turned on a vacuum cleaner.

Sal said, "Your son is the one they have for killing the teacher?"

While staring at her, Waverly pulled out a fat joint and slowly lit it, sucking on it, then blowing the smoke in her direction. Here, in this small space, with the tattoo up his neck, he looked far more dangerous than he had in her emergency department.

Sharon said, "He didn't do that. I think he was..I think he was getting..product from you a while back. I'm not here about that." She was aware she was talking fast, but they seemed to be listening. "This teacher, the one who died. She was investigating the whole drug thing. Taking pictures. Someone else may have been unhappy with her, wanted her dead."

She stopped. Aware the next logical words were, "Someone like you."

Sal said, "We are not killers." He looked at Jerome. "But she pissed off many people. Very stupid woman."

Jerome said, "My guess someone was sent to scare her off, you know, deliver a message, but the dumb fuck gets carried away. That's all."

Sharon said, "And who would have sent this dumb fuck?"

Jerome took a long pull, laughed, said, "You something else, Nurse Rat Shit. You something else."

Sharon said it again, "Who would have sent this person?"

Sal looked her over. "Who knows? Bikers, the mob, Toronto bosses?"

"Well, who was the teacher upsetting? Who was losing money?"

Sal said, "I think our visit is over."

Sharon said, "Look, I just want to understand. How it all works. Who might have been threatened by the teacher."

Jerome said, "Yeah, you should leave us, Nurse Sharon Gibson."

Sharon looked up at him, bit her lip.

Jerome said, "I know. They protect you in the hospital. Just your first name on that tag on your left tit. But you tell us your kid's name. Nurse Sharon Gibson. So now we can figure out where you live. *Comprende*?"

In the car heading home, aware it was now mid-afternoon, heavy traffic. Cell phone still in her pocket with her wallet. She checked. Her purse? No. She hadn't taken it to her visit at the detention centre. No purse. Breathe.

She had moved quickly when the tall one, Waverly, had threatened a home visit. And they hadn't stopped her when she jumped to her feet and headed for the door.

What the hell was she thinking?

And Alicia. Home all day alone. But probably on her phone. She pulled into the driveway and sat for a minute. There was little she hadn't seen as an emergency nurse, but this sordid stupid selling a puff of crack to teenagers through the eye hole of a door was...really stupid. She assumed it was crack. Yesterday's drug of choice. Now opioid overdoses were beginning to show up in emergency. Some pharmaceutical grade. Some concoctions from God knows where. Mixtures of shit. Amphetamines, oxycodone, benzos, fentanyl. Lethal combinations.

And how was this helping Christian?

And then she said aloud, "Sharon. You have a daughter at home. Go give her a hug and look after her."

# Twenty-One

There was a time Ben Walters would have known who to ask. Back then, nothing went down in this city without one of the two crime families knowing about it, giving the okay or not. And he'd just have to wait in the Five Star Café on James North an hour or two until the don came in to have his ring and his ass kissed. The old man, and then that hulking fat son of his after the old man died. The son who forgot how important it was to keep the peace between the families, just divide the spoils. There was enough to go around. Who would have guessed a whole town would be nostalgic about the Mafioso, the days a couple of Sicilian crime families controlled all the illegal activities?

And another rule the son broke: keep it in the family. Don't go outside the family hiring goons. Two good rules. But the son inherits the throne and hires a fucking addict to kill Johnny Papalia. In broad daylight, by the tennis court in the little park between Railway and Bay Street, this guy shoots him in the back of the head. How the hell this punk got Johnny Pops out of his house on Railway Street for a Saturday morning walk in the park, he'll never know. But he did.

Then the new don, Pat, he pays the shooter, Murdock, a couple thousand bucks and 40 ounces of cocaine when they meet up in the back of the Gathering Place the evening after the hit. Wood fire pizza joint the Musitanos owned on James, three blocks away from the park. Where they played Frank Sinatra music all day, you believe it.

And that was that. All downhill from there. The families go to war, lose control. The bikers move in, take over the drug trade in the east. The Asians. The Jamaicans. Maybe some Russians. And gambling? Shit. Big casinos open up down the street. Now legal, online, and off-track. The days of running numbers and renting out illegal slot machines were over. Still, there was what? Shipping, construction, trucking...

And who knew where the drugs were coming from now? You could buy the mixings legally, buy them online, set up a lab in the suburbs. At least for meth. Or bring the others in from China, buried somewhere in those shipping containers.

*You're an asshole*, he said to himself. *You come on to the lady, and then you fucking promise to keep looking into it. When her idiot son probably did it. None of the pros would have bothered. Maybe they'd knock off some competition in the alley behind King Street, but not a lady teacher in the high school. But criminals do some pretty stupid things. Shooting Johnny Pops was one good example.*

Walters was sitting in his home office, musing on this history, trying to figure out where to start. Teenagers using drugs. The supply coming from somewhere. The drugs being just what? Marijuana, stimulants, ADHD medications, cocaine, crack? Maybe the oxys. Still, the kid probably did it. Only a teenager would get that angry about a meddling teacher calling his momma. Unless she was threatening the supplier. And who but the kids would know their source?

He put his feet up, looked around his office, really a converted bedroom. It was one thing being paid to follow a philandering husband and taking a few photos, looking into some shady financial transactions. But the drug scene these days is a mess. No one crime family in control. Dozens of different drugs and combos, sources, sellers, dealers.

He couldn't think of anyone to call. The guys on the drug squad wouldn't give him the time of day. But, Christ, the lady is a nurse, and he had a soft spot for nurses, good-looking ones anyway, maybe from the days he wore a uniform. He took his feet off the desk, decided he'd give it a shot at least, go prowl around some of the shadier hangouts in town and see what turns up. Maybe find someone who owes him.

He parked in the lot behind Sam's Hotel and Tavern and walked around the corner down Chestnut to Barton, past a side entrance to something called Sam's Urban Lounge, an after-hours club of some sort, figured it must be basement level, under the tavern. At the corner, he paused a moment to take in the empty store fronts, boarded up, a wasteland of what was once a thriving working-class community in the shadow of the steel mills.

The city had gussied up the flowerbed down the middle of Barton, but it was like putting lipstick on a pig.

He stood outside for a moment, looking at the place. The sunlight faded. He checked his watch. Pretty early, but he was ready for a drink. Sam's Hotel and Tavern was a three-storey brick, rooms on the top two floors rented for the night or week. On the street level, the tavern. The building, he figured, circa 1920. Air conditioners crammed into windows, some windows boarded up, paint peeling on the sills and on some trim that was probably added in better days. He went inside, made his way past the tables, sat at the bar, asked for a bourbon on the rocks. Bulleit would do.

The place was filling up now, the bar stools getting crowded. He moved with his second drink to a corner table where he could see who was arriving. At first, just the all-day types, alcoholics who sat and nursed a drink, brooding over it. Maybe it was the junk and clutter of the place, the uneven lighting, the clatter and noise, the bits of conversation that made it feel like home. Not one of them looked like he would know the time of day, let alone what was happening in the supply chain for cocaine or crack. In one of the corners, a regular was having an animated conversation with himself.

A younger crowd started coming in later, some Asians, some Blacks. He didn't understand the appeal of the place for them, apart from free parking, and maybe being within walking distance of some banquet hall. He had planned to nurse one drink and then act like he'd downed three or four, hint he was in the market for something, see if that got him to someone who might know the talk on the street. But he'd come too early, and this was what? His third or fourth. Should have waited until maybe 11.

His mind wandered back to the mob days, remembering how they caught the shooter, Murdock, not even Italian. Maybe it was just a story, but the guy was not bright. After Murdock takes out the big boss of the other family, Johnny Pops, Pasquale Musitano, Pat, sends him off to whack the next in line, the guy running the Papalia family business in the Niagara region, a ways down the QEW. Story was this Niagara mob guy was big, tall, heavy. Murdock drives to his home, parks in the driveway, goes up to the door. The mob guy answers the door, opens it. Murdock steps in and right away pulls out his piece, says, "This is for Pat." And shoots him. The guy, you'd think he'd be more cautious answering his door, but it's a fatal shot, and he slumps back, falls against the front door, blocking it shut. And maybe it's a small hallway might explain it, but the story is now Murdock can't get back out the way he came in. The mob guy's body is blocking his exit, leaning against the door. So, change of plan. Murdock goes through the house to the kitchen, finds a window he can open, and crawls out. Halfway down the QEW heading back to Hamilton, he realizes he left prints all over the kitchen window. So he turns around to go back and clean them off. And he gets caught. Cops are already there. He knew there were holes in the story. Why the hell didn't he just leave by the back door? And how did the cops get there so fast? But it was a good story and mostly true. He did shoot the Niagara guy, and he did get caught.

Walters realized a lot of Black guys had come in now, most with women, some Asians, but they had filtered through the bar and gone down a flight of stairs in the back, leaving the regulars behind. A woman sat at his table, didn't say anything at first. Then she pointed to her empty glass and winked at him. He couldn't tell her age behind the heavy makeup, the damage done by alcohol.

He said, "Sorry." And got up. Decided it was a stupid idea in the first place and he might as well go home, but first maybe check out what was happening downstairs where the music was coming from. They were all fairly young going through and down, might know something. He made his way to the back, along the hall to the washrooms, and found the flight of stairs going down to the pounding techno beat. He guessed Sam's Tavern and Sam's Urban Lounge shared the washrooms.

# Twenty-Two

Walters saw a couple of other white faces in the crowd but otherwise this basement club was full of shades of black, brown, crew cuts and small beards, dreads, snazzy women, some hoodies and ball caps, some moving to the beat, the beat coming from a DJ in the corner. He made his way to the bar, asked for a bourbon on the rocks. With his drink in hand, he said, "Large crowd tonight? Or you get this all the time?" The bartender, a kid no more than twenty-five, said, "They come from a whatdayacallit, a celebration of life. For the guy got knifed a few weeks ago."

Walters said, "Yeah? That was the...?"

The kid said, "I don't know nothing about it." And went back to the other end of the bar.

Walters looked around. So most of these were friends, or family, or business partners of the guy got knifed, killed. Started in a barber shop, he remembered. The guy in there for a trim and the killers followed him in. Stabbed him there and followed him out on the street when he ran and finished the job. Papers said it was retribution for a smack down the guy gave someone outside a bar a few weeks before that. Supposedly all started with some disrespect. Jesus H. Christ. Grown-ass men behaving like teenage gangs.

Maybe drugs involved, or would-be hip hop artistes. Probably drugs. Same story. The two mob families self destruct and the field's left wide open. So the teacher got killed could have been any reason. Kid didn't like his grades, gonna call his parents and rat him out, some small-time drug dealer from Brantford didn't like her attitude, or some asshole felt disrespected.

He found a chair as far away from the speakers as possible. It was still too noisy to think. Another group was coming down the stairs from the tavern. Young, mixed, Black, Asian, maybe Arab. He never understood this urge to go underground, dance to music that hurt your ears, flashing lights that hurt your eyes, putrid air. Too many fucking people. Low ceiling. Terrible acoustics. Then he had an idea, just before the shooting started. Maybe it's like fairy tales. Fairy tales for young adults. These people want to get as close as possible to hell, visit hell, feel the horror, get dirty, and still be able to go home.

# Twenty-Three

Sal said, "I don't think this is working."

Jerome was still standing, looking at the door, twitching. "Yeah, you're fucking right this isn't working. What I've been saying. We spend the day in this shit-hole apartment, feeding stupid teenagers for five bucks a pull. What I'm telling you. We need to visit your friends."

Sal said, "No, amigo. I tell you never open the door. You open the door. Nurse goes to the cops, now they got cause. And you're using more and more, every day. I see it."

"And you got a plan?"

"Yes.

"Yeah? So, lay it out."

"It doesn't include you, *hommes*."

Jerome said, "It doesn't fucking include me? Your two-bit deal? Fuck me, you're a loser." He abruptly headed for the kitchen and the packet of powder on the table, waiting to be cooked into rock. He quickly spread out a few lines and snorted them. When he looked around, Sal was standing near the door, hands at his side. With a piece in his right hand.

Jerome said, "Ahh fuck. Little man's got a gun."

"I think it time you left. Go back to your momma."

Jerome was savouring the rush from cocaine and thinking he could take this little bastard, throw him out the window. But they were on the first floor. So drag him up to the roof and throw him off. Fucking little wog spic.

Sal moved away from the door but raised the gun, used it as a pointer, showing Jerome the way.

Jerome's hands were twitching, clenching. He was picturing Sal going off the roof, screaming, hitting the pavement. And it wasn't much of a piece. Fucking little pistol. Might not even shoot real bullets. But pointed right at him now.

Sal saw Jerome considering going for him, looking around for a weapon, tightening up. He said, "You take the last of the powder and go. All yours. It is, how you say it, your severance package."

Jerome looked over at the remaining powder. He moved quickly, stuffing it in his pocket, turned, stared at Sal for a second. Then, with a "Fuck this shit," he left. Walked past Sal to the door, pulled it open, went through and slammed it shut, all the while repeating, "Fuck this shit." Told himself he'd come back and shoot the little fuck and clean him out.

On the way home in his Honda, he wondered about getting rid of his momma. Not that she was doing anything for him, shit, and still probably high as a kite. Can't kill your momma, though. Maybe get her put away. He'd have to figure out her bank accounts first and see if her disability pension would still be coming.

And maybe find out where that cunt nurse lived and pay her a visit.

# Twenty-Four

At the door Detective Nash had said, "I have couple of questions. Can I come in to ask them?"

Sharon had looked him over, then said, "Why not?" She told Alicia to go to her room. She hadn't moved right away, not until Sharon gave her the "I fucking mean it" look. Then Alicia went upstairs. But probably just around the corner listening.

Sitting now, Nash said, "Look. It may be entirely unrelated to your son. But..."

"But what?"

"We have another homicide victim."

"You know where my son is, so why are you here?"

"The victim is a PI. Once was a cop, until alcohol finished him."

Sharon said, "The victim was a private investigator?"

Nash said, "Uh huh. And we found a piece of paper in his wallet with your name, address, and phone number on it."

Sharon said, "A private investigator." She sighed, said, "Ben Walters?"

"That's the one."

"Oh, Jesus. You said 'homicide victim'?"

"Uh huh. There was a shooting in a club the other night. You probably read about it. Saw it on the news. The Urban Lounge. Although lounge is a pretty fancy word for this place. What was Walters doing there?"

Sharon said, "What happened?"

Nash said, "We think he was collateral damage. Just happened to be there. Maybe looking for something, or who knows? That's why I'm here. Thought you might know why our Mr. Walters was spending his time in the Urban Lounge. It's a younger crowd in there, and mostly Black."

Sharon asked again, "What happened?"

Nash said, "Well, as far as we can tell, it goes back to a couple of other gang-related events. Most of the patrons that night were having an after-party. Clubbing after attending a celebration of life for someone got stabbed to death a few weeks ago. In come friends of the guys who killed him, friends of the two mugs who knifed the first victim. They shoot the place up. These assholes keep score, you know. Figure they have to even things out or they'll lose respect. And Ben Walters, ex-cop and PI, happened to be there, we think. No connection to this other shit. Not that we know of. Then we find your name in his wallet. That's why I'm here."

"I have no idea why he was there."

"And your name in his wallet?"

"Okay. I hired him, and then I fired him. I hired him to look into this thing my son has been charged with. You sure as hell weren't doing anything. I found his name. Through Google. Private investigators, Hamilton/Niagara. And I hired him to look into it."

"You fired him?"

"Right away he did something stupid. I fired him. But he apologized and told me he'd still look into it. I thought he was bullshitting."

Nash sighed, said, "He'd be over his head. Christ. He'd been doing divorce shit, mostly. Child custody stuff. And still drinking."

"So he got himself shot, killed?"

"Yeah. Someone else dead we think would be the real target, and a couple injuries."

"And so this one's my fault, too."

"Why would he be there, Sam's Tavern?"

"Sam's Tavern?"

Nash said, "Same place, one above ground. Just another dive. The upstairs catering to the drunk and unemployed, the downstairs catering to the younger crowd."

Sharon said, "Look. He said something about the street. Asking on the street. Finding out who in the supply chain might be really pissed at the teacher. She'd been doing her own amateur sleuthing, you know. Taking photos of the kids using and buying. I think she's got some of the dealers in the photos. Maybe. It was an idea."

Nash said, "And you know this because...?"

Sharon ignored the question. "Christian didn't do this thing. You should be looking somewhere else. Other motives. Like someone in the gangs doing it. Doing it because poor Ms. Teacher was cutting into their profits. Something like that. And if you don't mind, I have a shift tonight at the hospital."

Nash said, "Walters would be way over his head."

Sharon was standing now. "Well, excuse me. I tried to find Sam Spade, but he was fucking out of town."

Nash got up, headed for the door, said, "Okay, Mrs. Gibson. I'm sure we'll talk again."

When they were having supper, Alicia had said, "Where's your head at, Mom?" And now in the ER the intern had posed the same question. "Sharon, where's your head at?"

She had pulled herself back to concentrating on the case at hand. Another overdose with this new shit going around. Naloxone administered on site by the paramedics, the now-half-awake addict brought to emergency. For what? So he could be watched and given another dose if he slipped back into unconsciousness. Vital signs monitored. They'd give him breakfast and let him go in the morning. Back on the street.

This new stuff, fentanyl, bad enough by itself, but laced with God knows what. Benzos, animal tranquilizers. They actually had to be careful to not get exposed themselves, keep the masks on, gloves. Take blood, send it to the lab, monitor vitals, check in every fifteen minutes. Keeping the guy alive.

Sharon had said, "I'm okay. I just need to get this shift over and get some sleep."

She was thinking this new substance, imported from China, they were saying, made the stuff those two idiots were selling to teens look almost quaint. Cocaine and crack. Sure, you could use too much of the stuff, but a single inhalation wouldn't just suddenly make your heart stop. But this fentanyl. Taken by mouth or injected. A bit too much, and you died. She didn't understand it. Why? Why do they risk it? She had asked a few times. Most of the addicts just came back with the bullshit about stopping soon, going into a program. That was the last time. I swear to God. Then they'd be back in the next week. One had given her a sort of honest answer, she figured. He'd been homeless all winter, begging in the rain, car to car at the intersection, living out in the cold. Kicked out of a shelter because he'd been caught using. Overdosed on the doorsteps of the public library. When he was back with the living, she'd asked him, honestly puzzled. "It must be awful standing in the rain and sleet in January, begging for enough to get another fix. Why do you do it?" She must have worked up to that question, been taking his blood pressure at the same time. And he had told her it was worth putting up with the cold and wet for a few hours to get eight hours of bliss. She had repeated the word, "Bliss?"

"Yeah, bliss, you know."

"I don't know," she'd told him and then gone back to the coffee room.

# Twenty-Five

Jerome heard her talking before he opened the door. Just a drone of words. He assumed she was talking to the television, talking back to some televangelist or salesman. But when he was inside, he found she wasn't sitting in front of the TV. She was pacing, walking, moving her arms, sometimes pointing. And it wasn't just a drone of words. She was spitting them out, shouting, muttering. Hair a mess. Too much makeup. She looked exhausted, but still moving and talking. Now headed toward him. Cornered him before he could get through the hall to the kitchen.

She was in his face now, saying, "Jerome, honey. You know all about it, Jerome. You know. Be good to your momma, Jerome. I miss him so much. So much. And then there was this time, and again, and I didn't buy any this time, but I waited for you, Jerome, not like those others, those bastards and bitches, and bastards and bitches."

He grabbed her shoulders, said, "Momma. For Christ's sake. Where are your pills? Where are your goddamn pills?"

She pulled away from him, saying, "I don't need pills. I don't need any pills. I'm not mental. If your father were alive. I need, I need. Oh, to hell with it. I need your brother to be alive. You didn't kill him, did you, Jerome? Did you? Of course not. It was an accident. No one's fault. He drowned. That's all. My little boy drowned."

And then she swung back, turning quickly, a new face, a sudden change. "And you know I have the power now. I have the power to bring him back. If I pray every night. If I pray every night he'll come back to me, if the devil hasn't got him."

Jerome said, "Fuck. I'm calling the clinic." He reached for his cell in his left pocket, but his mother was all over him, backing him against the door jamb. He shouted in her ear, "And you've been drinking! Not taking your pills and drinking. Fuck."

Jerome took her arms, held her, pushed her back. She was singing now. Singing. Something. A hymn, some rock of ages thing. He should just leave. He headed for the stairs and up to his room, but she was on his heels, right behind him. Not singing now. Screaming at him. "Don't you leave me. Don't you dare leave me."

Jerome got to his room, but his mother was still behind him. What now?

He said, "I'll talk to you later, Mom. I'll come down and talk to you later. Just give me a minute. Let me shower and change."

He sat down on his bed, his hand going to his left pocket. But suddenly she was on the bed beside him, all over him, still talking, muttering, breathing, her hair even wilder, eyes fierce.

Then, a quick change to soft, near tears now, pleading, she said, "You know what I need, Jerome. You know what I need. You know what I need."

Her hands were groping at him. Her face told him what she needed. And that's when Jerome hit her. He hit his mother. Hit her in the face with his fist. She reeled back in shock, her nose starting to bleed.

Jerome got to his feet quickly, while his mother still sat, mouth open in shock, blood coming fast now. He fled the bedroom, down the stairs, out the front door, slamming it behind him, shouting fuck at the sky, a long agonized, "Fuuuck."

He should call the clinic, get the nurse to come, Mary, get his mother to the hospital. Tell them she came on to him. Fuck. The image troubled him, disgusted him. What she wanted from him. Christ. And he broke her fucking nose. Broke his mother's nose. Hit his own mother. They come, they'd see that, and ask, and he'd tell them, what? What the fuck would he tell them? She fell on her face, hit her nose. And she wouldn't let me phone. So I had to leave. I had to leave her.

Jerome sat on the steps. He pulled out his cell and found the number of the clinic. He tapped on the screen. When someone answered, he asked to speak to Mary. The voice told him they had two Marys working there. He said, "I don't know her other name. A nurse, comes to see my mother, Waverly. I'm her son, Jerome. She's in a crisis."

The voice told him Mary was seeing someone, in a session, she'd relay the message. And if it's an emergency, you should call 911.

Jerome tapped again, closed his phone, sat staring at the road in front of the house. He couldn't hear his mother in the house. Maybe she was calm now, quiet. Still in his bedroom. He took the package of powder from his pocket, sprinkled some on the back of his cell, snorted it, put the package back in his pocket. He saw the leaves of the maples change, move, the sun breaking through the clouds. Some older lady walking a dog on the other side of the street. He dialled 911. Found himself talking rapidly. Told them his mother was psychotic, mental, in the house, hurting herself.

She's bipolar, manic. A patient, been in the OH before. Must be off her meds. The operator asked for his location. He told them his address, said he'd be waiting outside.

The cocaine was working now. Getting ideas. Get her off to the OH, then get power of attorney, get some cash, get back in business. Feeling a bit of excitement. He waited, kept sitting, his leg twitching, let his brain go with the blow, watched the leaves move, reflect sunlight, watched the odd car go by, the woman with the dog get to the end of the street, turn and come back.

An ambulance arrived, stopped right in front of the house. The driver and an attendant got out, a paramedic. A police car pulled up behind the ambulance. That's when Jerome remembered the package in his pocket. The paramedic was talking to him now, asking if he was the man who called, "Are you Jerome?"

Jerome nodded, said, "She's inside. Upstairs, I think."

Then the cop stepped up to him, asked if there were any weapons inside. Any guns? Jerome, still sitting on the step, shook his head. "And anyone else inside? Just your mother, right?"

Jerome said, "She needs to be in the hospital."

One of the cops entered first, the lady cop, then the paramedics. The other cop stayed outside, standing on the sidewalk, looking across the street at the small crowd gathering. Jerome sat as still as he could, his head buzzing, his left leg jiggling a little.

The lady cop came out, passed Jerome and stood by the other cop on the walkway, talking to him, both looking across the street. Jerome couldn't hear what she was saying. The second cop, the male, slowly turned and walked over to the foot of the steps, looked at Jerome. He said, "Your mother says you hit her, broke her nose."

Jerome said, "I pushed her away. I pushed her off me, that's all.

She's fucking crazy."

The cop said, "Are you using?"

"What?"

The cop said, "You look like you're on something."

That was the moment, as Jerome remembered it, that was the moment the blow took over, short-circuited his brain. He got to his feet, now towering above the cop on the sidewalk, and told him, told him his mother was crazy. "She's the one. Take her to the hospital. You didn't come for me. I'm the one called. fucking cops. Do your fucking job."

The cop was unfazed, asked him to empty his pockets.

Jerome said, "Fuck you."

And then the lady cop called for backup.

Resisting arrest, breach of probation, possession. That put Jerome back in a cell block in the detention centre, awaiting a court appearance. But at least they took his momma to the hospital where they'd keep her a while.

A day or two, then sober and remorseful, he goes before a judge. Tell him how stressed he was, looking after his very sick mother. Bipolar. Really crazy that day. He'd be let out with conditions, maybe have to see his probation officer more often, attend a program. But at least he'd have the house to himself, and time to figure out his next move.

But anybody on the range asks why he's back in, he won't tell them he punched his mother. That would put him on the list with the pedos. It was the code. No matter you're a crack head junky felon, you don't hit your mother. And he wouldn't tell them she came on to him either. That was fucking weird.

# Twenty-Six

Pulling into the driveway, Sharon realized she was exhausted, that she had barely made it through her shift, and maybe, until Chris was home, she shouldn't be working at all. But then she'd have to ask Hamish for financial help, and she sure as hell didn't want to do that. Maybe she could talk them into giving her half shifts.

And she feared she was losing her empathy, at least for the alcoholics and addicts, and some of the stupid ways people get themselves hurt.

Maybe she just needed more sleep. She took a minute sitting in the car. An early summer morning, just after 8, already getting hot in the sun. She realized Walters was on her mind. Stupid, stupid bastard. But she felt guilty about it. If he was in those dives trying to get some answers to help her. Then...

Aloud, she said, "No. No. No." And then grabbed her purse from the passenger seat and got out of her car.

Sharon put her key in the front door lock, but found it was already unlocked. Alicia, Jesus. But Alicia wouldn't be up this early. Maybe she came in last night and left the door...Or she'd been in such a rush herself, and distracted, she hadn't locked it when she left for work.

Once inside, Sharon carefully locked the door, trying it twice, then again, recognizing the touch of OCD that arose when she was stressed or tired. She took a step and stopped. She could see Alicia now, sitting in an armchair in the living room, facing her. Just sitting. Not still in bed as expected. Not at the kitchen table. Not on her phone. Just sitting there. Sharon was about to call out, ask if she's all right, what's going on, but she saw Alicia's eyes were open, conscious, alive, but her eyes moving to her left and flicking back.

Sharon took two steps into the living room, past the cabinet of family mementoes, looked to her right, and there he was. One of the men from the apartment, not her ER patient, the other one, the shorter one, just sitting in the armchair opposite Alicia.

Sharon put her purse down on the small table to her left, and the man said, simply, "Hard night at work, Nurse Sharon?"

Sharon turned back, willing herself to be calm. She didn't know his name, couldn't remember what the other one called this one. She said, "It was, actually. You probably know about this fentanyl shit that's going around. They're all overdosing on it. Then a head injury, two old ladies from nursing homes, one appendix, one broken arm, and a half dozen cuts."

He said, "No knife wounds, heart attacks?"

Alicia was staring at them, mouth open now.

Sharon said, "Oh yeah, a couple of heart attacks, but I don't remember any knife wounds."

Alicia said, "Do you know this, this...?"

Sal said, "We are acquainted."

Alicia said, "He rang the doorbell, and when I opened the door, he like just barged in, pushed his way in, took my phone from me. Mom?"

Sharon sat on the edge of the couch. She was tired, but she was also remembering her training, her experience: assume a non-threatening position, don't tower over anybody. She said, "And of course, there were some high fevers, abdominal pain, one serious asthma attack, one status epilepticus, and then this old homeless guy came in because he hadn't been able to piss in 24 hours. Had to be catheterized, but then drained slowly or we'd put him into shock. A prostate thing. Something you'll be acquainted with, some day soon."

Alicia was staring at her. "Mother, what are you doing?"

Sharon kept her eyes on Sal, said, "And to what do we owe the pleasure of your visit?"

Sal said, "You are something else, you know that? Something else."

Sharon said, "Actually, I'd like you to leave. If you were delivering a message, you've succeeded."

Sal looked her over, then turned his gaze to Alicia, said, "You have a very lovely daughter, *Señora*."

"I'm aware of that," said Sharon, but she was having trouble controlling her voice. "I'd still like you to leave."

Sal said, "I came by to give you this. I believe it belonged to your boy, Chris, right?" When he brought his right hand up, it held a knife. A knife, Sharon noted, that looked like the hunting knife she had last seen in Chris's room a year ago.

Alicia let out a gasp or a muffled scream. Sharon said, "Leave it and go."

Sal said, "Nothing gets to you, Nurse Sharon, eh? You are one cool chick."

Sharon said, "You're getting to me. You are definitely getting to me. Just leave the knife if you want, and go. Get out of my fucking house."

"No," said Sal. "I stay awhile, maybe have breakfast, no?"

Sharon said, "The knife had a sheath."

Sal looked at her, puzzled, "A sheef?"

"A leather holder thing, with a loop goes on the belt."

Sal said, "You cover your fear very well, Nurse Sharon."

If he stood up with that thing in his hand, Sharon didn't know what she'd do. But he was still sitting. She said, "Why do you have that thing? And how do I know it belonged to Chris?"

He stood up then, holding the knife at his side.

Sharon fought the instinct to run, knew what she should do—what she'd learned from the shrink at the hospital, had seen it work. She had watched two cops bring in a man, escort him to the isolation room. Then they waited outside until the shrink finally arrived. He had talked to the cops and then knocked on the door, introduced himself and asked if he could enter. He waited for a yes and then opened the door. She could see the man, the patient, now pulling a small knife from some pocket the cops had missed. And the shrink still walked into the room, giving him a wide berth, and sat on the floor against the wall on the far side. This image flashed through her mind.

She slid carefully off the arm of the couch and settled lower on the cushion. He looked puzzled by this move. She said, now looking up at him, "Where are you from, originally?"

He looked at her, sat back down, shook his head and shrugged, said, "El Salvador."

Sharon had to keep this going. Changing the script, the shrink called it. She asked, "Are you a landed immigrant or a citizen here? And is that the knife that killed the teacher, because I thought the police had it?"

She had taken the conversation right back to the knife. Stupid. But how do you get back to immigration policies or the weather?

Sal said, "The police do not have a murder weapon."

"And you know that because...?"

Sal said, "I think you know the answer to that question."

Sharon turned to Alicia. "I'm sorry, sweetie, I'm sorry. It's my fault we have this...visitor." And then back to Sal, "I get your message. You know where I live with my daughter. I know about your operation on Upper Wentworth. I won't talk to the cops about it. Just leave the knife and go. Please."

"We understand each other?"

But she couldn't let it go. She had to know. "Did Chris trade you that knife for drugs, pot or something, months ago?"

Sal said, "You ask too many questions, Nurse Sharon. Perhaps you do not fully understand."

Sharon said, "All right, all right. I do understand. I fully understand. Just leave it and go. Or keep it and go."

Sal said, "Does your daughter understand as well?"

He was staring at Alicia now. Leering at her. "Perhaps she could come and work for me, do some cooking. Alicia." He lengthened the *cia* of Alicia in a Spanish accent.

Later, Sharon thought that was probably the moment, hearing this creep say her daughter's name in that seductive fashion. The moment she threw aside all her crisis resolution training and turned to a different approach. She scanned for a weapon, got to her feet unsteadily, all the while talking, saying, "Maybe when she's sixteen. But she's too young now for a part-time job. Aren't you, Alishiiiaa?" Then, "You two get acquainted while I make some coffee." She started for the kitchen but faked a stumble, tripping on a dislodged pillow. She stumbled forward, reaching out to steady herself. This brought her within arm's length of the one Inuit carving she owned, a soapstone bear on the prowl sitting on the lower shelf of the open cabinet. Sal looked puzzled. Alicia screamed. In one motion, Sharon's right hand swept the carving from the shelf and into the left side of Sal's head. He had started to raise his right hand, with the knife, but the bear was heavy and hit its target. Sal looked at her, eyes wide, then he slumped, slipped out of the chair onto the floor, some blood running down his cheek. The bear landed on the floor, one leg snapping off.

Sharon was looking at the bear. "Fuck." The one valuable piece of art she had. Then she looked over at Alicia, said, "Get something quick. To tie him up. In case he comes to. The lamp cord will do. Come on."

Later, talking with the police, and with her adrenalin still high, Sharon told them all she could think about at the time was the value of the bear, maybe close to five thousand dollars now, that, and a memory that intruded. A stupid memory from years ago, a news item, when the prime minister of Canada used an Inuit carving to hit an intruder. "Do you remember that? Jean Chrétien, I think." She took a breath, willed herself to stop talking.

Sal had regained consciousness to find his hands and feet bound with a lamp cord, and Sharon sitting in a chair above him, the broken soapstone carving in her hand, ready if needed.

Sharon knew when the cops took this intruder away with a

head injury, they'd have to take him to the hospital first. Check for concussion, or worse, an internal bleed. She asked, "Will you be taking him to the General?"

The cop had answered, "Yeah, the trauma centre."

And she had said, "Can you, this time, maybe take him to St. Joseph's? They can check him out there just as well."

The cop looked at her. She said, "I work there, The General Hospital. I don't want..." Then she trailed off, not knowing what she didn't want, and turned to look after Alicia, who was staring at her mother as if she were the intruder.

# Twenty-Seven

Sharon called the hospital, told Personnel and the Department of Nursing she needed a week off to look after her daughter. Maybe two. They compromised on one vacation week, one week of sick leave.

She didn't let Alicia out of her sight that first week, shared her queen-size bed, found herself checking the locks and the windows several times a day.

Alicia vacillated between, "Mother, you have to stop hanging out with lowlifes." and, "You were like She-Hulk in there. Are you secret CIA or something?"

Sharon had answered, "More like Ellen Ripley, I think, protecting her kid."

Alicia had said, "Who?"

It was midway through that week when the lawyer, Tony, called Hamish, and Hamish called Sharon. Chris was being released. They didn't have enough evidence to go to trial. Sharon added, "And they have another suspect."

"How do you know that?"

But Sharon was not going to tell her ex about her and Alicia's visitor. Not yet. Not now. She simply said, "I've talked with the cops, the detectives."

"What did they tell you?"

"They have a small-time drug dealer in custody. A man with a record."

Hamish had asked, "Do you understand any of this?"

Sharon had told him, "Not really. Chris was doing drugs, just pot, I think, I hope. And he was selling to his friends. And he had some dealings with this guy they've got in custody now. Darnell, the teacher, I think she was going to warn me. Chris was skipping class. Maybe she thought he was in some kind of danger, or something. And she was on a crusade, sneaking around taking pictures of the kids smoking, buying. I don't know. I just don't know."

"You don't know what?"

"Why somebody killed her. But she had pictures of some drug buys, snapshots. Maybe she had something really incriminating."

Hamish had asked, "How do you know this stuff?"

And Sharon had simply answered, "The cops talk to me."

Hamish had said, "Not to me they don't." Then, "Well, as long as we get Chris home."

With Alicia in the front passenger seat, Sharon had driven her Jetta to the detention centre, circled the entrance, and had stopped opposite the side door she had been told Chris would emerge from. Alicia had asked, "Do you think he'll have some prison tattoos? Like on his arms and neck?"

And Sharon had answered, "If he has, I'll strangle him myself."

She pressed the button on her car door to let the two front windows down. A nice breeze entered, but so did noises and fumes from Barton Street. The General Hospital was just two blocks down, and, a little farther along the other way, to the east, she knew she would find Sam's Tavern. She worked in this neighbourhood, but it had never occurred to her to take a stroll, go outside the hospital for coffee, drop into the Crowbar Café. She recognized that as a nurse, in the hospital, on her home turf, she could be kind, sympathetic, treat everybody the same, be non-judgmental, as they say. But there were limits. There were fucking limits.

A correction officer came out the door they were watching and stood to one side. Then Chris emerged. He was wearing the clothes Sharon had brought him, just pants and a shirt, and carrying a paper bag. Presumably with his toiletries.

He looked around, saw the car,and walked toward it. He was tall and thin. He looked like he'd lost weight. Sharon stepped out of the car and he continued toward her, not rushing, not celebrating, not making eye contact. When she took him in her arms, he was stiff at first, then he shuddered and wept. Alicia joined the family hug.

For the ride home Alicia switched to the back seat, leaving the front for Christian. He seemed unsure of himself, contrite, staring straight ahead. During the drive, Sharon tried to make conversation, ask some questions, but she couldn't find any small talk that made sense. And Chris wasn't responding anyway. He clutched his paper bag, turned his head away, and stared out the window.

They pulled up in front of the townhouse Hamish owned, an address Sharon knew but had never visited. Chris said, "Why are we here?"

Hamish had been watching for the car and was now coming out the front door. Still in the car, Sharon said, "Christian, I love you, but you're going to be living with your father for a while."

"What?"

"For a while. You'll visit us. Just reversed for a few months, that's all."

Chris was looking at her now, said, "Mom. I didn't do it. I swear to God."

Sharon sighed, said, "I know. I know. I sincerely hope...No. I know you didn't do it. But you need your father. You need your father, now. I'm sorry. And please...And please don't say that phrase again. Don't use it. Just don't use it."

"What phrase?"

"'I swear to God.' I don't want to hear that phrase ever again. Please."

On the drive to their home, Alicia now back in the front passenger seat, she asked, "What's going to happen now? I mean, like..."

Sharon took her hand, squeezed it, said, "Just us girls, sweetie. Just us girls for a while."

Alicia said, "Mom. Two hands on the wheel, please."

Printed in Canada